I0671786

Highland Dom

McMillan Passion

by

Marie Tuhart

Highland Dom

Contact Information: info@thewildrosepress.com

Cover Art by *Diana Carlile*

The Wild Rose Press, Inc.
PO Box 708
Adams Basin, NY 14410-0708

Visit us at www.thewilderroses.com

Publishing History
First Scarlet Rose Edition, 2018
Print ISBN 978-1-5092-2171-4
Digital ISBN 978-1-5092-2172-1

Published in the United States of America

Let the negotiations begin...

"Look at me." His command was just as firm as his last. When their gazes met, he let out a breath. "How much do you know?"

"You volunteer at the local BDSM club, and teach sexual health at the university." Her voice was soft and low.

"Yes, but how much do you know about the lifestyle?" Was she really interested? It was hard to tell.

"A bit." She squirmed in her chair. "This isn't the place we should be talking about this."

Cam glanced around the café; no one was here, yet. And his sister was keeping to the kitchen. "No one is here. Tell me."

"I..." Her gaze dropped, and she shook her head. "Not here." Her voice was stronger. "I won't risk my business."

Someone walked by the café, and Cam shifted in his seat. "Meet me for dinner tonight."

"I have to bake tonight."

"I'll bring dinner here, but we are going to talk." Cam stood up and circled behind Kristen as someone walked into the café. He leaned down and whispered in her ear, "Because I can't wait to tie you to my bed. Tease you. Torment you. And take you." Cam straightened, turned, and strode out the café door.

Dedication

To my critique group: Isabel, Nia, and Chandra.

To the Editing Maven, who helped me whip this book into shape.

Chapter One

Cameron McMillan strode down the sidewalk of his hometown of Grant, Washington. The crisp, late January morning air tickled the hair on his arms. He was a man on a mission. He wanted to surprise Kristen. She hadn't been far from his mind in the last six months that he had spent teaching in Scotland as a visiting professor. He'd arrived home from Scotland yesterday and had spent his first night with his family. His mother still hadn't forgiven him for missing Christmas with the family. Today, he'd see Kristen and settle once and for all if she was interested in a relationship with him.

He glanced at his watch. Three minutes after six. Her café, Cozy Corners, would be open. University classes didn't start for another week, but the students had started moving into the dorms and local houses. The café wouldn't be too busy yet, but in the next few hours, he'd be lucky to find a seat. Cameron pushed open the glass door. The smell of fresh coffee and blueberries tickled his nose.

"Hi there, big brother," Skye whispered as she leaned forward from her place behind the counter, giving him a sly grin and a wink.

"Hi." He kept his voice low. The last thing he wanted to do was tip off Kristen he was there. He wanted her to be surprised at his appearance. Skye had informed him Kristen didn't expect to see him for a few

1

days.

"I'll get your drink and scone, and I'll tell Kristen someone is here to see her."

"Thanks, Skye." Cam sat at the small table in the corner to wait. Skye delivered his coffee and scone before she disappeared into the back.

He made quick work of the scone, loving the light texture and the sweet blueberries. Kristen's blueberry scones were the best; he'd missed them while he was in Scotland. Another reason to come home…at least for a little while. He had an open invitation to return to Scotland in six months, and he was thinking about it.

But first, he wanted to see how this attraction to Kristen played out. He had no idea if she was still interested in him or if she wanted anything to do with the lifestyle.

"Those fritters have to come out in five minutes." Kristen's clear voice echoed in the empty café.

Cam kept his gaze on the doorway to the kitchen area, waiting for Kristen to appear. He was rewarded as she walked out, her brown hair pulled into a ponytail that bounced with each step she took. She maneuvered around the counter, revealing her "Kiss the Cook" apron over a pair of jeans. He grinned, thinking about grasping her confined hair, tilting her head back, and ravaging her mouth. As a Dom, he loved ponytails.

She studied a piece of paper in her hand before setting it on the counter and looking up. Her eyes widened in surprise. "Cameron." His name came out in a breathless rush.

"Hi, Kristen." He stood, his libido taking notice of how delicious she looked this morning.

"You're home."

"Yes, come and sit down." He gestured for her to have a seat at the table. He inhaled the subtle scent of cinnamon. Her green eyes sparked with curiosity and a bit of wariness. "Umm, I've got fritters in the oven."

"Yes, and Skye can take them out." He took her by the elbow and guided her over to the table, waiting until she took her seat before resuming his.

"You're home early." She shifted in the chair, looking more nervous than relaxed.

"Only by a week." He sipped his coffee, hoping to get her to relax.

"Well, welcome home." She gave him a warm smile. "I'm surprised your mom isn't making you a big homecoming breakfast." She motioned toward his empty plate.

"We had a family dinner last night, but today, I wanted to see you."

"Me? Why?" She tilted her head. He almost stood up to move behind her and press his lips to her exposed, slender neck.

"We have some unfinished business." He reached across the table and captured her hand before she could pull it back. *Almost.*

"We do?" Her voice trembled a bit as she sat straighter in her chair.

"Yes. Did you really mean what you said at my going away party?"

Her teeth nibbled at her lower lip for a minute and damn if his dick didn't grow hard at the action. "What did I say? That was six months ago." She lowered her gaze to the tabletop where he held her hand.

"You remember." He squeezed her hand then lowered his voice. "Look at me."

When she didn't move an inch, Cam inhaled deeply, reined in his dominant side and said, "Please, look at me."

She lifted her gaze from their hands to meet his. Her eyes were wide and bright. "Cameron," she started, trying to pull her hand from his.

He didn't let go. "Tell me. Did you fantasize about me tying you up in my bed and having my wicked way with you while I was gone?"

A blush rose to her cheeks, and she wiggled in her chair. "I shouldn't have said that to you."

"So you *do* remember?" His dick pulsed.

Her lower lip disappeared into her mouth for a moment. "Yes, I remember. I was inappropriate that night."

"How?" He took a sip of his coffee with his free hand to cover up his eagerness at her answers.

"Come on, Cameron. I don't have to tell you I was tipsy. I never should have cornered you in the hall at your going away party and whispered those words in your ear." A light blush took over her cheeks. "I was impulsive that night, and telling you I wanted you to tie me up was inappropriate."

"Are you saying it's untrue?" Had he come back for nothing?

"No!" The word burst from her lips. Her cheeks turned a darker pink. "Yes…oh, crap." She tugged her hand free and put them both up to cover her face.

Cam could only smile. She was interested in him, definitely. Interested in the lifestyle, maybe. "Kristen, take your hands away from your face. There's nothing to be ashamed of." His voice was firm yet gentle.

Her hands fluttered to the tabletop, but her gaze

stayed lowered. A submissive in the making? His groin tightened as his blood warmed. She would be good for him, an eager pupil.

"Look at me." His command was just as firm as his last. When their gazes met, he let out a breath. "How much do you know?"

"You volunteer at the local BDSM club and teach sexual health at the university." Her voice was soft and low.

"Yes, but how much do you know about the lifestyle?" Was she really interested? It was hard to tell.

"A bit." She squirmed in her chair. "This isn't the place we should be talking about this."

Cam glanced around the café; no one was here yet, and his sister was keeping to the kitchen. "No one is here. Tell me."

"I…" Her gaze dropped, and she shook her head. "Not here." Her voice was stronger. "I won't risk my business."

Someone walked by the café, and Cam shifted in his seat. "Meet me for dinner tonight."

"I have to bake tonight."

"I'll bring dinner here, but we are going to talk." Cam stood up and circled behind Kristen as someone walked into the café. He leaned down and whispered in her ear, "I can't wait to explore this attraction we have. Fully explore." Cam straightened, turned, and strode out the café door.

****

Kristen Caldwell gripped the table as Cameron walked out and a customer walked in. She couldn't breathe; hell, she could barely think. Cameron was home. The last six months had been torture on her as she waited for Cameron to return from Scotland. She didn't have an interest in any other man. It didn't help she'd had a little too much to drink at his goodbye party, and the wine had loosened her tongue enough to blurt out her fantasy about him. Part of her regretted saying the words and another part didn't.

But now he was home, and he hadn't forgotten what she'd said. Her stomach turned over, and it wasn't because she hadn't eaten yet. Her nerves trembled from his words, anticipation tingled beneath her skin, and a healthy dose of trepidation filled her mind. Her attraction to Cameron hadn't wavered in the six months he was gone. If anything, it had grown stronger and she wanted to explore the attraction with him.

"Cameron gone?" Skye asked after helping the customer.

"Yes." Kristen forced herself out of the chair, and back behind the counter. Skye was a good friend to her. Did Skye know about her brother's lifestyle? She had never mentioned it, but then again, she had never asked. Kristen slipped into the kitchen and began fixing the mini quiches after the fritters were put in the warming oven.

Thank goodness, she could do this in her sleep, because she couldn't get her mind off of Cameron's words. He wanted her in his bed. Tied up in his bed. She really hadn't expected him to come to her café his first morning home.

Part of her was thrilled he came to see her and another part was a little apprehensive. She'd agonized for months about what she said to him that night of his going away party. But Cameron was different. He hadn't brush her off, nor put her down. Maybe it was because he taught sexual health at the university. She'd heard his students talking in her café about the class. How Professor McMillan taught them about sex, self-pleasure, how to please a man and a woman, sexual diseases, and alternative lifestyles. Plus, he belonged to the local BDSM club. A club she longed to walk into, but her fear of being judged held her back.

A shiver of anticipation running up her spine made Kristen roll her shoulders. Despite her fear, she was drawn to BDSM. She so wanted to explore the lifestyle. The few times she'd tried it had led to disastrous results. But she trusted Cameron.

Over the years, she heard his students talking about his classes, how he championed alternative lifestyles, allowing the students to form their own opinions. He encouraged them to explore but to be safe about it and was willing to help any of them if they wanted or needed it.

She saw how he was with his mother and sister. Her lips curved up at the old adage. "You can tell how a man will treat a woman by how he treats his mother or sister."

Four years ago, she'd shed her family name and her old life when she moved to Grant. Her ex and her family were toxic, and she was finally happy. Now at thirty-two, she was free to explore. She had a feeling with Cameron it would be totally different.

This morning just proved her right. He hadn't gone all dominant on her although she'd seen the flash of dominance in his eyes. Her body and mind had melted. She'd read about BDSM—had done her research—and knew she had submissive traits within certain limits. After her ex, she had learned she needed to define those limits, because she still wanted to maintain control of her life.

She'd had enough of her control being taken away by her family. She'd never let anyone have total control over her or her decisions, even if it was the super sexy, dominant Cameron. She had her limits.

"Hey, Kristen." Skye's voice pulled her out of her thoughts.

"What's up?" Kristen checked the mini quiches and pulled them from the oven.

"Mrs. Watkins is here about a cake for her daughter's birthday."

Kristen set the quiches to cool and washed her hands before going out front. Time to be owner and baker. She could think more about Cameron later.

Chapter Two

A knock rattled the bakery door at seven p.m. Kristen glanced up from the cake design book she was reading to see Cameron dressed in jeans and a polo shirt, carrying two plastic bags. She stood and ran her hands down her apron then opened the door for him.

"Hi," she greeted. Her skin tingled with anticipation.

"Hi." His right hand slipped around her neck, holding her still as he gave her a light kiss. "You taste like vanilla," he said before letting her go.

Kristen let out a laugh. "Vanilla cupcakes are in the oven." Her nerves danced in excitement at his kiss and touch. She hadn't expected that kiss.

"I have dinner." He held up the bag in his left hand.

The scent of beef teased her nose. "Is that what I think it is?"

"Burgers and fries from Maxine's."

Kristen's stomach let out a growl, and Cameron laughed. "Someone is hungry."

She relocked the door and led him toward the back. "We'll need to eat back here, or people will be knocking on the door, wanting treats." She waved Cameron toward the table in the corner.

Slipping on her oven mitts, she opened the industrial oven door. Yep, cupcakes done. She slid the pans out, setting them on racks to cool before putting a batch of mini cakes in to bake.

"Why don't you hire someone to do all the baking for you?" Cameron asked, standing next to the table.

Kristen set the timer and turned to him. "I like baking. It makes me feel good. Besides, this is my business, and I don't want to hire someone to do it. Skye comes over in the mornings to help. Plus there's Tim, who helps with the customers."

"Yes, but you still work sixteen hour days." He glanced around the kitchen.

Kristen was proud of her kitchen. She had a prep area away from the ovens, large work tables, and plenty of room even with several ovens and refrigerators.

"Sometimes, I have long days, and other times, I don't." She did work long hours, but only because she didn't have a life outside her business. But maybe now…she was ready for things to change.

She grabbed napkins out of a nearby cabinet and glanced over at Cameron. "Do we need plates?"

"Blasphemy, woman." He let out a laugh and began pulling the big Styrofoam containers out of the bag. The scent of the fries caused Kristen's stomach to growl again. "When was the last time you ate?" He tossed a couple dozen ketchup packets on the table.

She removed two bottles of water out of the fridge and set them and the napkins on the table. "Hope water is okay. I can make coffee, and there is some soda. My beverage delivery arrives tomorrow morning."

"Water is fine." He slipped around her and held her chair out.

Her breath hitched in her throat at his closeness before she sat down.

"You didn't answer me. When did you last eat?"

Cameron's breath brushed her ear.

His husky, firm tone sent a shiver through her bloodstream. "This morning, I think." Cameron moved away, and she let out a breath. Her nerves were hyperaware when he was near.

"You think?" He stared at her as he sat down. "You need a keeper."

"Are you applying for the job?"

"Damn straight." He tilted his chin toward her box. "Open it and eat."

Kristen opened her mouth to tell him she was joking, but his pointed glare had her swallowing her words. She opened the container and let out a sigh of pleasure. Maxine's burgers and fries were legendary in Grant. She lifted the bun, and surprise hit her low in the stomach. The tomatoes and onions were missing.

"No tomatoes, no onions, cheddar cheese instead of American, cooked well-done with lettuce and mayo," Cameron said, his gaze still on her.

"How did you know?" She picked up her burger and took a bite. Her eyes closed in bliss as the flavorful beef melted in her mouth along with the sharp tang of cheese.

"You've eaten at enough of our backyard barbecues."

"That doesn't mean you should remember how I take my burger." She squirted a couple packets of ketchup onto the lid of the box and swiped her fry through it.

"I remember everything."

Kristen swallowed her fry. *Everything?* Her nerves fluttered in her stomach, and she stared at Cameron. "Like what?"

Cameron's blue gaze fastened on her face. "Like…you take your coffee with cream and sugar, lots of sugar. You won't eat strawberries, but you'll eat blueberries. You've only dated two men since you came to Grant. And you never talk about your past."

Holy crap, he paid attention. More than she realized. She set her burger down as her stomach turned over. She didn't talk about her family, but something could have slipped out. She hadn't monitored every conversation she had in his presence. What else did he know? But then again, she was the one who'd made the comment about him tying her to his bed and having his way with her.

"Don't stop eating." He took another bite of his burger while watching her.

With a sigh, she picked up her food and began eating again, wondering what else had he'd noticed.

Cameron cursed silently as a wall came down between him and Kristen, cutting him off. He needed to watch his step with her. The last thing he wanted to do was scare her away, but she needed to understand he wasn't going to pussy-foot around.

He was a dominant. And if he was going to be her dominant, then she would learn quickly that he would make sure she took care of herself. No more skipping meals. And honesty. He had to have honesty.

His ex, Julia, hadn't been honest with him, and that had almost ended in tragedy because of Julia's deceit. He pushed away thoughts of his former submissive. Last he had heard, she was doing great in Chicago, enjoying life with a new Dom, an old friend of hers.

He looked across the table at Kristen. Her dark brown hair was pulled back away from her face, and her green eyes sparkled with curiosity as she polished off her hamburger. He allowed his gaze to wander from her face to her breasts.

He remembered them as being nice and round from last summer when he'd seen her at the pool, but now they were hidden by her shirt and bra. How soft would her breasts feel? His fingers itched to find out. *Not yet*, he reminded himself. He couldn't rush. He needed to take his time with her, so he forced his impatience away.

Kristen wiped her hands and mouth on her napkin before pushing the box away from her. "I'm stuffed."

"There are still fries." Cameron had already polished off his meal. He'd have to run an extra mile tomorrow to work it all off, but nothing beat Maxine's burgers.

"I'm full, Cameron." She sat back in her chair, arms crossed over her chest as she glared at him.

He shook his head. "You don't eat enough." He'd noticed that when she came to the house for meals with Skye.

She frowned at him. "I eat all I need." She stood up and began clearing the table. She took the mini cakes out of the oven only to put another batch in.

"Are you going to bake all night?" he asked.

"No. That's the last batch."

"Good. How much time do we have?"

"Twenty minutes."

"Sit back down." He gestured to her chair and waited until she sat. "Why did you approach me six months ago, Kristen?"

She closed her eyes then opened them. "Because Skye had mentioned you'd broken up with your girlfriend. I wanted to see if the spark between us was real or a figment of my imagination." She rubbed her palm over her nose. "Plus, you were leaving for six months, so if I had made a fool of myself, we wouldn't have to see each other on a daily basis."

Cameron let out a laugh. "Kristen, we've been seeing each other almost daily since you opened Cozy Corners. I was one of your first customers."

"Yes, you were." She smiled at him.

Damned if his cock didn't leap to attention just as it had done since the very first day he ventured into her café. She had smiled at him when he had walked in the door. His libido had woken up, and he still wanted more.

"How much do you really know about BDSM?"

Her cheeks flushed, and she sat up a little straighter in her chair. "I've dabbled."

"Dabbled how?" Had she played at a club? Been in a full-time relationship?

"A few times at a private club and some with my ex-fiancé."

Ex-fiancé? Was that the bad relationship Skye had mentioned four years ago? "One of the items I insist on is honesty. I need to know your history, your wants, your desires, and your fears if you want me to be your Dom."

"I do want you as my Dom, and I have limits." She clasped her hands together.

He hadn't read her wrong; she was ready to take this step with him. "Hard or soft?"

"Hard limits."

He nodded; she knew some of the terminology, so she wasn't a total newbie. He liked that. "You can spell them out to me later." He leaned forward.

He had asked her for honesty, and he could do no less than return the favor. Maybe if he opened up to her, she'd open up to him. "To clear the air, my last girlfriend was actually my submissive. We parted company because she lied to me."

"I see." She closed her mouth then opened it, only to fall silent.

"You can ask me anything." He couldn't deal with lies anymore. After Julia's lies, his confidence as a Dom had taken a hit. At thirty-six, he was getting too old to play games. Well, certain games.

"Okay, I don't see," Kristen said. "But if she lied about something important, I can understand why you would break up."

"That's why I need honesty in all things. About your life, how you feel when we're playing, and when we're not. If I do something that upsets you, tell me. I want to know everything, not just what you think is important. That is a hard limit for me. Can you be honest with me?"

She sat back in her chair, her arms crossed over her ample breasts. "Will you explain about her?"

"Yes, but not today." He wasn't fully ready to discuss Julia with her yet. But he would because he owed Kristen honesty as well.

She nodded and blew out a breath. "I will be honest about my wants and needs," she said. "About my time here in Grant, and my sexual history, but my life before Grant is off limits. I never really lived until I moved here."

Interesting. Cameron wondered what she didn't want to discuss from her past. He could live with it for now. He'd get the full story out of her later. "I can live with that unless not sharing starts to impact our relationship."

"Agreed."

He stared at her. Her eyes were clear and bright. She wasn't frightened but not exactly open. But then, what did he expect? This was new for her, and she was distracted by work. They needed to spend some quality, quiet time together. "Let's talk about schedules."

"Well, you know I work quite a bit."

"Yes, and in order for this to work, you'll need to devote some time to us."

"I can cut back. What do you have in mind?" She sat back in her chair, starting to relax. It was a good sign.

"Classes start next week, so my days will be filled with teaching. Can you take two week nights and the weekends off?" He was pushing her. While he wanted a submissive, he also needed someone who would express their wants and needs. Was he testing her? Maybe. He knew she worked some long hours with her café…too long.

"Well…" She shook her head.

"Kristen." Cameron leaned forward, putting his elbows on the table. "This will only work if you put the time into it."

She glanced down at her lap, then back to him. "How is this going to work?" The timer beeped. Kristen stood up and took the cakes out of the oven.

Cameron bit back an impatient sigh. He was moving too fast. He needed to give her time to get used to them being together, something he'd been thinking about for the last six months. She set the cakes on the cooling rack before resuming her seat.

Cameron smiled. "We can make it work. Communication is the key. You need to tell me if I'm overwhelming you or pushing you too hard."

"I can do that." There was a wary note in her voice. "Give me time to think and work out a schedule. I can have something by this weekend."

He nodded. "You said you dabbled and went to a club?" He wanted to know more about her experience.

"Private club—well, sort of." She puffed out a breath when he just stared at her waiting for her to continue. "Okay, here's what happened. I dabbled at nineteen with a boyfriend. Then there was my ex-fiancé who thought I was a deviant for wanting more than the missionary position. I've read a lot of books about the lifestyle, both fiction and non-fiction."

"Erotic romance?" He knew it was popular. Hell, his sister devoured them.

Kristen nodded.

"Romance is the fantasy with some truths in it." He leaned forward. "Tell me about the private club. Was it actually a club or in someone's house?"

"The first one was at someone's house. But another time, we went to a rented, industrial space." A tremor swept through her, and all of Cameron's instincts went on high alert.

He reached across the table and put his hand over hers where it rested. Her gaze met his, and she gave a small smile. "I was very uncomfortable. Too dark, too noisy, too many people."

"Were there monitors?"

"If there were, I never saw them. With the noise level, even if someone did scream out their safeword, no one would have heard them unless they were standing really, really close."

Cameron nodded. He'd seen parties like she described. "I've been to parties like that, and I've walked right out. I believe in the safe, sane, and consensual." While Kristen had knowledge of the BDSM world, she didn't have the complete experience. It sounded like the club she'd gone to was filled with wannabes instead of actual community members. "I want to show you my world—the safe, sane, and consensual BDSM world that I enjoy."

"I want to try with you." Her voice had a hopeful tone to it.

"I do, too." And he did. "I want a relationship with you and kink will be a part of it." When she didn't say, anything he continued, "Since it's Thursday, can you take tomorrow night off?"

"Yes." She turned her hand under his, and he entangled his fingers with hers. His blood sang when she didn't pull away from him.

"Tomorrow night I want you to come to my house for dinner."

She shifted in her seat. "Okay."

Cameron grinned. "Don't look so apprehensive. I won't do anything you don't want to do."

The tension left her face. "Do you want me to bring anything?"

"Just yourself." He squeezed her hand before releasing it. "I need a piece of paper and a pen."

She jumped up, found what he wanted, and handed it to him.

He quickly wrote down a couple of websites before handing her the paper. "I want you to look at those websites, and read up on what is there. I'll pick you up tomorrow night at seven."

Cameron stood, and so did Kristen. "What should I wear?" she asked.

"Whatever you want. This will be our first date."

Her eyes widened.

She wasn't expecting that from him. He had made his attraction to her clear, and now was the next step. Dating and kink.

"Are jeans okay?" There was a slight tremor in her voice.

"That's fine." He ran his finger over her cheek, pleased when she leaned into his touch. Cameron slipped his hand behind her neck, tugging Kristen forward. "I expect more of this." His lips covered hers in a gentle but firm kiss.

Her mouth was warm and soft against his. He was careful to nip and lick at her lips playfully, not to demand too much. Her body relaxed against his as he slipped an arm around her waist, holding her close.

When her lips parted and her tongue touched his, Cameron couldn't resist. He slipped his tongue inside her mouth, taking his time, tasting her sweetness before tangling with hers. He kept his touch firm on the back of her neck but not constraining.

Kristen's arms lifted and entwined around his neck as the kiss went on and on. His kiss grew hard, then back to soft. He nipped at her lips before taking her mouth again, their tongues tasting and playing with each other.

He lifted his head, and she gulped in a big breath. He chuckled before dropping a kiss on her nose. "You taste so sweet. I want to gobble you up." His lips slid over her cheek to her ear, nipping at the lobe.

"Cameron." Her fingers tangled in his hair.

"Read the websites. Tomorrow night if you're up for it, we'll have some fun." He bit her lobe again before stepping out of her embrace. He turned toward the back door. "Lock up behind me."

Cameron waited outside to hear the lock click. "Good girl. See you tomorrow," he called out.

A sense of pride filled him. She was an independent woman and didn't need a man to make her feel whole, and yet she had allowed him to take control without a struggle. His nerves danced with excitement. Kristen was going to be the perfect sub.

Chapter Three

Another yawn escaped Kristen's lips the next morning as she stood in the café's kitchen. Cameron had done that to her. After their explosive kiss, she'd closed down the kitchen and gone up to her apartment. She had gone to bed late, and once there, she'd tossed and turned.

She had fired up her computer, and she'd started at the top of the list Cameron had left for her. As she read each and every one of those explicit websites, her mind had reeled with questions and as well as a healthy dose of wariness. Some of the protocols and rules were so not her style.

When she did finally fall asleep, she had dreamt about Cameron. Him tying her up, or flogging her, or…a wave of desire flooded her as she remembered those dreams made her wet and wanting. She covered her mouth as she yawned again. Thank goodness, there were no customers in the café.

Kristen turned to Skye. "Hey, are you okay with opening tomorrow?"

"Sure, I've done it before." Skye squinted at her. "Did you have trouble sleeping last night?"

"Sort of. I was restless."

"Did my brother have anything to do with that restlessness?"

"Skye." Kristen's hands fluttered as her face

flushed.

"Oh come on." Skye threw her a grin. "Cameron has liked you for a long time, but neither of you were ready for a relationship. But now…I think it's great."

"Nothing is going on." Not yet. But what would happen after tonight?

"When are you seeing him again?"

"Tonight." Kristen's head snapped up, and she stared at Skye. "You tricked me."

"Me?" Skye grinned.

"Don't get over excited. We're just testing the waters."

"Well, I'm glad." Skye sauntered away.

Kristen retreated to the kitchen. What was she thinking? Cameron taught sexual health at the college. Would students and faculty think she was obsessed about sex? Would they think she was obsessed with BDSM? And what about the rest of Skye's family think about her and Cameron being together? Oh hell, what would her customers say? Her stomach clenched; her ex-fiancé called her a freak. Would others think she's a freak? Would they make snide comments behind her back? Her heart was beating so fast she could barely breathe.

Maybe this wasn't such a good idea. She took her cell phone out of her pocket and sent a text to Cameron, telling him she'd changed her mind about tonight.

Five minutes later, her phone rang.

Cameron. "Hi."

"We're still on for tonight, but there's a slight change of plans." His whiskey-smooth voice soothed her nerves.

"Cameron—"

"No running, Kristen. We're going to explore together, even if it means I have to kidnap you and keep you tied up."

"You wouldn't." Now why did his words send a shiver of anticipation rather than fear through her veins?

"Don't test me."

"What's the change in plans?" Maybe dinner someplace public would be better.

"Mom wants me at dinner tonight. I told her I had plans with you, and she said to bring you along."

"You told your mother about us?" Her voice rose, and she winced. Oh hell, she'd barely acknowledged to Skye that she was dating Cameron, and he had told his mother? This was going to hell in a hand basket.

"Sweetheart, my family loves you. This will be like any other dinner at my folks' house."

"But they know we're seeing each other."

"Yes, so that means if I kiss you in the kitchen or grope you under the table, no one will care."

"Cameron, be serious." Her stomach knotted. "What if they don't approve?"

"Is that what you're worried about? Unbelievable."

Kristen's spine stiffened. He didn't understand. She wouldn't be able to stand it if his family didn't approve of their relationship; she'd had enough of other people's disapproval in her life. Tears filled her eyes. "I'm sorry, Cameron. I...I can't do this," she whispered.

"Ah, shit." His voice grew low. "Kristen. Sweetheart. It will be okay. You have to know that. My parents are not going to disapprove."

"You can't know that."

"I'll pick you up at six thirty. No arguments. We'll discuss this then."

"But—"

"No buts, Kristen. See you tonight."

The line went dead, and she blew out a breath. Well, that was a colossal fuck up. Now Cameron was upset because of her. Why couldn't she just tell him about her parents? She snorted. How could he understand the hell her parents had made of her life? He had a loving, stable family. Hers were bat-shit crazy.

She put her phone away and glanced at the clock. Ten thirty. She'd better get to work. She had a lot of baking to do since she would be taking the night off.

****

In his playroom, Cameron paced. Why would Kristen think his parents would object to them dating? Something wasn't right. This was a big issue for Kristen, and they would work it out. He couldn't iron out every issue between them in the first few hours of their relationship. He wanted to give her time to tell him without pressure from him. He shook his head. He'd get to the bottom of it later. Right now…he glanced around his private space.

Even though he'd played at a club while in Scotland, he'd missed having his own room for private playtime. His brother, Alec, had taken care of his home while he'd been gone.

Sometimes, Cameron wondered how he and his brothers had all become involved in BDSM. In his case, he'd always been curious, and sexual curiosity was just another rung on the ladder.

In high school, he had found sex education fascinating. He was intrigued how the human body worked and so much more. So he had taken science classes that focused on physiology. When he'd decided to go to college, he focused on the body until one of his professors suggested he start looking into sexual health.

A whole new world had opened up to him. The more Cameron had learned, the more he wanted to teach others. Not only about heterosexuality, but also about homosexuality, alternative lifestyles, and loving your body and yourself.

Everyone had sexual drives. Sometimes, the sex drive was depressed or underutilized, but everyone had one. Even Kristen.

What was she afraid of? Her concern about what his parents would think had thrown him for a curve. His parents loved her. Didn't she realize that? Maybe not, based on the conversation they'd just had.

Cameron grabbed a cloth and began cleaning the room. How many times had she'd been over for dinner? Countless. Hell, she'd been at his going away party.

She had to know his family thought the world of her. His family had kept him informed while he was in Scotland. Skye had loved to tell him that Kristen wasn't seeing anyone, even mentioning when customers had flirted with her. Had Kristen waited for him? He'd like to think so.

While Scotland had been good for him, both personally and professionally, his reasons for going still haunted him. Julia's half-truths had made him doubt himself as a Dom. He'd regained his confidence, but he worried about Kristen.

He'd expressed his desire for complete honesty, and she'd put her foot down on her past before she came to Grant, he wondered why? Was she worried he wouldn't understand?

Something about her family made her wary. He would find a way past that wariness. But tonight, he'd show her the man he was. How much he wanted a relationship with her and how much his family adored her. Maybe in doing that, it would boost her self-confidence, and she could be more comfortable around him.

Chapter Four

Kristen paced around the café kitchen. Cameron would be here any second, and she couldn't get out of going to his parents' house.

Tira McMillan, Cameron's mother, had called her that afternoon, telling her she was so happy she was coming to dinner. No one said "no" to Tira. Kristen couldn't go empty-handed, so she'd told Tira she'd bring her favorite dessert—mini cakes. It didn't matter that they'd sold all of them that day. Kristen had whipped up a quick batch and put them in the oven. She'd finished decorating them right before it was time to close the shop up for the night.

Kristen had run up to her apartment, had taken a quick shower, and had changed clothes. Where she might have worn jeans to Cameron's place, she wouldn't to his parents' house. She slipped on a light, broomstick skirt and a pretty, lacy blouse.

She texted Cameron, instructing him to come to the back entrance to the café. It would make loading the cakes into his car easier. Because she was such an overachiever, she'd made eight cakes, one for each person at dinner—Cameron, his parents, Skye, his three brothers, and of course, herself.

A knock on the back door caused her to jump, and she hurried over to it. "Who is it?"

"Cameron."

Kristen undid the heavy-duty lock and pulled the door open. "Hi." He looked absolutely delicious in the button down dark blue shirt and black slacks. His dark hair was neatly combed, and his blue eyes were bright.

"Hi," he replied and swept her into his arms.

His mouth settled over hers. Kristen melted as he nipped at her lips until she opened them, allowing him full access. His tongue swept inside as her arms crept to his shoulders before curling around his neck.

Heat started in her core and began spreading through her veins. His tongue dueled with hers, sweeping over the roof of her mouth and then her teeth. His arms tightened around her waist as he pulled her closer. When he finally drew back, she gulped in some air, a little dizzy from the excitement of being in his arms.

His fingers were tangled in her hair. "I needed that," he whispered.

"Damn, you can kiss," she said, trying to catch her breath.

"Just wait," he whispered, his mouth next to her ear, "until I have you beneath me, naked."

A flush rose over her face in a hot wave as she shifted from one foot to the other trying to quell her arousal. "Your parents are expecting us."

Cameron let out a breath. "Yes, they are, but I won't always let you off the hook so easily." He released her.

She forced herself to take a step back from his magnificent body. His chest was firm and his arms strong. If she let herself, she would sink back into his embrace.

He cleared his throat. "Mom said you offered to

bring dessert."

"Yes." Kristen pulled herself together. *Dinner. His parents. Dessert.* "Over here." She strode to the counter where eight boxes were lined up.

"Are we feeding an army?"

Kristen let out a laugh. "You forget I've dined with you and your brothers before. You have big appetites."

"Some bigger than others." He snapped his teeth at her, and she shook her head.

"Behave." She handed him two boxes, while she grabbed two. "Let's load these into the car."

"As my lady wishes."

Five minutes later, they were on the way to his parents' house. Kristen twisted her fingers together in her lap.

"Are you still nervous about what my parents will think about us?" Cameron asked.

"Yes. You just came back from Scotland. It's not like we've been in a relationship or anything."

"Honey, anyone who had witnessed that kiss you gave me six months ago wouldn't be surprised you were one of my first stops."

"But…" *Oh, shit.* She remembered that kiss she'd given him. Right after she had whispered in his ear about him tying her up on his bed and having his wicked way with her, she'd laid a big kiss right on his lips. She hadn't thought about anyone else seeing them in the hallway, kissing. Embarrassment filled her.

"No one in my family is judging you."

"Everyone judges," she muttered. "And I'm always lacking." It was a festering wound inside her thanks to her parents. It didn't matter what she'd done; it was never good enough. She wasn't good enough.

29

"Who the—" Cameron cursed and whipped the vehicle to the side of the road.

"The cakes!" she exclaimed as he pulled the car to a rough stop. "Did we hit something?"

"No, and screw the cakes." He slammed the car into park and ripped off his seat belt before turning to her. His blue eyes were a turbulent sea, and a nerve ticked in his clenched jaw.

"Cameron?" She was puzzled why he pulled over so abruptly.

"Who the hell told you that you were lacking?"

If his eyes didn't give her a clue to how upset he was, his voice certainly did. "It's not a big deal." She looked down at her hands clasped in her lap. Old fears welled up in her. What would Cameron think of her? Would he find her lacking? Her heart clenched at the thought.

"That's a lie. Honesty, remember?" A warm palm cupped her chin and turned her face to him. "You are not lacking in anything, and anyone who has said so has very bad judgment."

While his words warmed her heart, her brain reminded her of past mistakes. Going to the BDSM party with a boyfriend, then confessing her needs to her ex-fiancé. She had lost some of her dreams, but not all of them. "Cameron, I've come to terms with it."

At least, she thought she had. After her grandmother died, the knowledge her family would never support her choices had caused her to leave and change her last name. She didn't want any association with them. But old feelings simmered to the surface.

She cleared her throat. "We're going to be late for dinner, and you know your mom hates tardiness."

He studied her for a minute. "I don't like leaving this to fester. You will tell me why you feel this way eventually. But no one in my family will judge you, and neither will I. You are special and unique." He released her chin and refastened his seat belt.

Kristen's heart pounded at his words. Her world brightened; maybe she could relax and be herself. Cameron pulled back onto the road and began discussing how crazy his life would be in a week when classes started. She smiled and nodded, happy to have a mundane conversation with him as her mind processed his words about being special and unique.

She drew in a deep breath when he pulled up to his parents' home. Their home always did that to her. She loved the McMillan house—two-story colonial with a wraparound porch. The faux stone made it look older than it was. She remembered how Tira had told her about driving the contractor nuts because she'd wanted everything just right.

Kristen pushed the car door open and met Cameron at the rear of his vehicle. He frowned at her, but she chose to ignore it.

Ian, the youngest brother and in college, came bounding out of the house and down the stairs, stopping next to Kristen. "Hi ya, doll." He pressed a kiss to her cheek. "What's cooking?"

"I'm good, Ian. How are classes going?" She reached into the trunk.

"Okay. Let me help you." He took two of the boxes she pulled out. "Be right back."

"Scamp," Cameron muttered.

"He's just being helpful." She pulled two more cakes out and waited for Ian to return.

"He wants your cakes."

"And you don't?"

"What I want—" Cameron started.

Ian returned. "Mom says to hurry up, dinner is ready." He slipped the boxes from Kristen's hands and took off for the house.

Kristen picked up the last two boxes, unsure if she was happy that Ian interrupted Cameron or not.

Cameron closed the trunk. "We better get in there before she sends out a search party." He gestured with his chin to the front door.

She started up the walkway. Tira was waiting by the door.

"Kristen, honey, you outdid yourself as always." She took one of the boxes from Kristen.

"It was nothing." She admired Tira's reddish brown hair pulled back in a set of elegant silver clips.

"I know better. Skye told me you baked them especially for us," Tira said.

"Skye is a tattletale," she muttered.

Cameron laughed. "You're just figuring that out?"

"Smart ass," she whispered as his mother led them down the hallway.

"This from the woman who wiggled her ass all the way into the house." He pushed the front door shut with his foot.

"I did not."

"Be careful, or I'll spank it."

"Promises, promises." She sashayed down the hall to the kitchen to tease Cameron. What had gotten into her? She never flirted with anyone like that. The thought brought her up short. Why did she feel so comfortable with Cameron? Maybe because he'd told her she was special. No one had ever told her that, and he allowed her to be herself. Kristen spied a grin on Cameron's face before she made her way into the kitchen.

"Let me take those," Tira said as she took the boxes and set them on the counter.

Cameron walked in a minute later, and his mother turned and enfolded him into a hug. It didn't matter that he was more than six inches taller than her. A wave of envy swept over Kristen. Her mother had rarely hugged her, had barely shown her any attention. If it hadn't been for her grandmother, she would have had a childhood devoid of love.

"I'm so glad to have you home," Tira said. "We missed you at Thanksgiving and Christmas."

"I'm happy to be home, Mom."

Kristen went across the room to talk to Skye, letting son and mother have some privacy. "You told your mom about the cakes," Kristen said.

"Was it a secret?" Skye's face filled with concern. "I didn't think…"

"It wasn't." She smiled.

Skye's eyes lit up. "You're teasing me?"

"Yep." A weight lifted from Kristen's shoulders. She didn't feel judged here. The family accepted her as they always had. She has a future here, with her café, friends, and maybe with everything Cameron could offer her.

Tira clapped her hands. "Let's get a move on. Dinner is waiting."

****

Several hours later, Cameron started his car and pulled away from his parents' home. Dinner had been lively and good. Before dinner, he had been glad that Kristen had been talking to Skye when his mother told him there would be no talk about him going back to Scotland. She had missed him while he was gone.

He assured his mother he hadn't made his decision yet, and talking about it over dinner wasn't an option. He hadn't said anything to Kristen yet about possibly going back. He wanted to see how this attraction between them played out. He was hopeful they had a future together. The lure of Scotland was there. The university had offered him a nice salary if he would teach there, and there was much more sexual freedom, but it didn't have Kristen.

"I'm so stuffed," Kristen said. "Your mom's roast beef always comes out so tender."

"She's a wonder in the kitchen." Cameron reached over and took Kristen's hand in his. "And your cakes were a big hit. How did you manage to bake eight different cakes this afternoon?"

"It wasn't hard." She glanced out the window.

"From someone who can't bake worth a crap, I think it's pretty miraculous." She seemed somber, and he wanted to lighten the mood.

Her laugh in response was light, and it went straight to his dick. He wanted to hear more of her laughter.

"How did you get into baking?"

The change in the air was instant. She started to pull her hand from his, but he tightened his hold. Why was she so defensive? He hadn't asked about her family.

"Cameron," she started.

"Why are you upset? Don't freeze up on me. I just

want to know more about you."

"Sorry, the question surprised me." She shook her head. "I took up baking because it was fun, and I enjoyed it."

Cameron pondered her answer then decided to try another track. "Tell me about your ex-boyfriends and ex-fiancé."

"That's even worse."

"You promised me some sexual history." He glanced over at her. "If we're going to explore kink together, it's something I need to know."

"Damn," she whispered. "What do you want to know?"

"How many boyfriends?" He'd start with the simple stuff.

"Before or after high school graduation?"

"After. I'm sure they had no clue what they were doing before." Most teenage boys didn't. They were more interested in getting their own pleasure.

"You're not kidding there." She shifted in her seat. "My first boyfriend after high school was more into impressing my parents than me, so he was dumped quickly."

Now that was an interesting tidbit about her family life. She didn't seem bitter but matter of fact.

"After that, I didn't date for a while."

"Why not?" Were the boys blind? How did they miss seeing the sensual creature inside Kristen?

"Because I wanted someone who wanted to be with me."

Cameron mulled this over. She was dropping little clues. He'd put them together as he got more of the pieces. "What about your next boyfriend?"

"Karl." She bit out his name like it was poison.

He glanced over at her. Her jaw was tight, and her lips pressed together.

"Not a pleasant memory?" What had the man done?

"No."

"Another one who wanted to kiss your parents' ass?" He might need to hunt this one down and make him pay for hurting his Kristen. His gut tightened. Yes, he considered Kristen his already.

"I wish."

Cameron pulled his car behind her café, turned off the engine, and turned to her.

"Well, good night." She reached to unfasten her seat belt.

Cameron caught her hands. "You're not getting out of this talk that easily. I'm coming in."

"Damn male," she muttered, and all he could do was grin.

He followed Kristen up the stairs to her apartment, thinking about the man who hurt her. He wanted to beat the crap out of the man and soothe her bad memories away. His reaction made him pause. She'd gotten further under his skin than he'd thought. Not that it was a bad thing. It just meant he would need to watch his reactions around her. A kinky relationship was new to her, and the last thing he wanted to do was scare her away.

Kristen unlocked the door, pushed the door open, and stopped for a moment before stepping completely inside. The first thing he noticed was a lamp was on. Was someone in her apartment? He grasped her upper arm.

"What is it?" She glanced up at him.

"Did you leave the lamp on?"

"Yes. I don't like returning to a dark home." Her gaze went to his hold on her arm and then back to his face. "You thought someone else was here?"

"A woman living alone can't be too safe."

"True. Which is why I have an alarm system." She jerked her chin back toward the door. Cameron glanced over his shoulder. So that was what she had done; she disarmed the alarm using the keypad when they'd entered. "Would you like some coffee?" she asked.

"I'm fine." He released her arm and shut the door. Her living room was laid out nicely with a beige sofa and overstuffed chair. A big, colorful throw rug covered the floor. A TV was tucked against one wall, and bookcases lined the other.

"Have a seat." She gestured toward the sofa.

"So…Karl?" he asked as he settled on her sofa in her apartment.

"Karl was a bit self-centered, but he liked to tie me up."

"During sex or other times?" Was that her first time with kink? He suspected it was.

"Both. He was the one who took me to a couple of kinky parties. The private parties."

"Where you felt unsafe?" He hated she'd experienced BDSM in a bad light. There were some who didn't care how they portrayed the community. It's amazing that such an experience didn't sour her on the whole kink aspect.

She nodded. "The first one wasn't so bad, but it was the last one he took me to."

"Did you play at these parties?" He needed to

know her history, she knew the right words, but as she'd mentioned, she didn't have a lot of practical experience.

"Depends on what you mean by play." She looked away from him then back. Her eyes clouded with apprehension. "At the first club, I allowed him to tie me to a St. Andrews Cross. Just tie me to it. No flogging. Nothing bad happened, but I didn't like how people looked at me."

Cameron curled his hand around her neck, caressing her tense muscles. "Tell me."

She shivered. "I felt dirty. They stared at me like I was a tiny morsel for them to feed on." Her voice shook. "They wanted to touch me, and I protested. They made me feel unclean, as if I was only there for their amusement. Karl threatened to strip me as I struggled."

"Did he?" Damn wannabe. Now he really wanted to go after the idiot and show him what humiliation really was. Cameron slid closer to her on the sofa.

"No." She blew out a breath. "It was just a threat."

"And the other party?" He continued caressing her neck.

"Because I didn't feel safe, I wouldn't allow him to tie me up or anything. We had a big fight after that party and…" Her spine stiffened, and she closed her eyes.

"What happened?" If the bastard had hit her, he'd hunt him down and make him wish he'd never been born. He closed his hand over her clenched fist.

"I don't know how it happened," she whispered, "but apparently, someone at the first party had taken pictures of me tied up. Karl was pissed at me, so he sold them."

The sorrow in her voice told him there was a lot more to the story. He waited patiently while caressing her neck and stroking the back of her hand, letting her know he was there for her.

"When they first came out in the tabloids, I really didn't care."

"What did your parents think?"

"Oh, they yelled and got angry, but then I could never please them, so it didn't bother me too much." She glanced up at him.

The tears in her eyes did more than pull at his heart. They made him angry. Furious that someone had hurt her so much, that the pain was still with her.

"What hurt more," she said, "was that I lost my chance to attend classes at a private pastry school. All the media hoopla was too much for them, and they asked me to leave."

"I'm sorry, sweetheart." He pulled her against his chest. Baking meant so much to her. Losing out of a special school must have wounded her tender heart.

"It's not your fault." She snuggled against him.

"How old were you when this happened?"

She tipped her head back. He was happy to see the tears gone. "Trying to guess my age?"

"I know how old you are."

"Really?"

"The same age as my sister, thirty-two."

"And you're thirty-six."

"Right." He dropped a kiss on her nose. "So how old were you?"

"Twenty-one, old enough to know better."

Without thought, he nudged her until she was sitting in his lap. "I don't agree that you were old enough to know better. He took advantage of you. What about the next boyfriend?"

Kristen scrunched up her nose at him. "Do we really have to do this?"

"Yes. We're not going any further in our relationship until we get the baggage out of the way."

"Will you tell me about your last submissive girlfriend?"

He froze for a minute then nodded. "It's only fair." He hadn't talked to many people about Julia, but he would tell Kristen. She deserved to know.

"Now?" The tone of her voice sounded hopeful.

"Later. Tell me about boyfriend number three."

"Boyfriend number three was also fiancé number one and an ass wipe."

He smiled at the derision in her voice. "Tell me how you really feel."

Kristen let out a little laugh and rested her head against his shoulder. "Part of me wonders why I didn't see through Brian."

"Another one who wanted to impress your parents?"

"Yes, but also, he was too perfect."

"Tell me more." He wanted to know what she meant by too perfect.

"You know"—she waved her hand in the air— "perfect hair, perfect teeth, perfect smile. Fake, totally fake, in more ways than one." She shifted in Cameron's lap. "Was it wrong for me to ask for a little kink in the bedroom?"

"Hell, no." What had this Brian done? Was this guy why she was so nervous about approaching him?

"Brian had called me a freak."

Cameron's arms tightened around her shoulders. Why did people who didn't understand the lifestyle want to label those in it? Even as a sexual health professor, he'd run into attitudes that had made him grit his teeth, which is why he pushed to educate more people. "So you broke up with him?"

"Eventually. We ended up engaged first."

"What the hell?" Cameron couldn't believe she'd actually been engaged to the jerk.

"I know. I'm such a pushover." She touched his cheek. "He didn't call me a freak until later. But that wasn't the worst he did." Her eyes closed. "The rat bastard took most of my money and then sold his version of our relationship to a tabloid."

A pattern was forming. While she didn't want to talk about her family, it was apparent her parents had some sort of social influence if the tabloids were so interested. Men had used Kristen to gain favor and for access to her money as well.

"And then," she said as a twinge of sadness colored her voice, "because of the story, I lost the job I'd fought tooth and nail to get. It was the last straw."

"Did your parents believe you were the victim?"

She let out a bitter laugh. "You've got to be kidding. I was the troublemaker. No one ever listened to me." She shook her head. "Okay, that's not right. My grandmother listened to me. She held me while I cried and told me not all men were bastards."

Cameron's arms tightened, and he cuddled her close. He was glad she had at least one person in her court. "You're not a troublemaker." His lips brushed her temple. "You are a beautiful, tempting woman."

"You are an irresistible, sexy male."

Her words sent a shaft of heat to his groin. "I seem to remember you resisting me for several years." He tilted her chin up, pleased to see her green eyes were clear and bright.

"I had a business to set up and get off the ground. I wasn't in a position to deal with a man. Any man." She brushed his hair away from his forehead. "I'm sorry it took me so long to realize I was attracted to you."

He allowed her to change the focus to him. "No worries." He nuzzled her ear. "Julia and I had a unique relationship."

"You said she was your submissive."

"Yes. I wasn't looking for a long-term relationship, but wanted a woman who would be my submissive."

"You found that in Julia?"

"I thought I had. Do you know what a masochist is?"

"Someone who enjoys pain." She tilted her head closer to his lips.

"Yes." He buried his nose closer to her skin.

"Are you a sadist?"

"No." He inhaled and enjoyed the smell of her skin, fresh without any artificial perfumes. Just Kristen. "That was the problem. Julia is a masochist, but I'm not a sadist."

"From everything I've read about masochism, I'm surprised you two got together."

"Julia told me she was fine with me not being a sadist. I'm not saying I didn't flog her or use a cane, but I'm not into causing pain for pain's sake. I want to give pleasure to my submissive. Hell, to any submissive."

"Of course not." Kristen's fingers trailed over his chest. "What happened?"

He'd made her promise to be honest, so he could give her nothing less. "I thought we were doing well. We'd been together almost three years when I found out Julia was cheating on me."

"What?" Kristen sat up straight in his arms. "Oh, Cameron, that woman had no idea what she was giving up."

His lips turned up in a smile. "Thank you." He dropped a kiss on her cheek. "Julia's cheating was in the sense of the lifestyle. She was seeing another Dom on the side, who would beat her the way she wanted." He took a deep breath. "She was able to keep it a secret by not seeing me for several days after seeing her other Dom, waiting until the marks had faded."

"It doesn't excuse what she did." Kristen huffed out a breath. "She had to take responsibility for what she did and why she had lied to you."

"I agree."

"Is that why you went to Scotland?"

"Partly." He shifted Kristen so he could look into her eyes again. "I needed a break to sort out my feelings, not only about what had happened, but the lifestyle."

She tilted her head. "Were you thinking about getting out of the lifestyle?"

The concern in her eyes warmed his heart. "No. I needed to understand the lifestyle from a different perspective."

"Going to Scotland did that for you?"

"Yes. They are much more open and accepting over there, and it reinforced my beliefs in the lifestyle."

"And yet here you are with me."

"Yes." He put his forehead against hers. "Because I

want to be. I've waited a long time for you." And it was true. His relationship with Julia had been doomed from the beginning. But he wouldn't let that happen with his relationship with Kristen.

"Me, too."

Their lips met. Her mouth was soft and pliant. Cameron forced himself to keep the kiss light and easy. He didn't want to scare Kristen, although he suspected she wouldn't scare too easily now that they had talked.

He lifted his head, releasing her sweet mouth. "It's getting late." Cameron lifted her to her feet and stood. "Did you free up tomorrow afternoon?"

"Yes. Skye is actually going to open in the morning for me. I'll do some baking and take the afternoon off."

"Good." With her hand in his, he walked to the front door. "Tomorrow, we'll explore your needs and wants."

"What about yours?"

He smiled. "Mine as well, but something tells me we'll be compatible." He drew her into his embrace, loving how she fit in his arms, her nose level with his lips. He kissed it softly. "I'll be by to pick you up at one tomorrow."

"Okay." Her arms tightened around him. "Are you sure you don't want to stay longer?"

"Don't tempt me." He brushed another soft kiss across her lips. "As much as I'd like to, we need to take this slowly. You have some knowledge but no real experience."

He'd like nothing better than to spend the night in her bed loving her, making her come from his fingers, his lips, and eventually, his cock.

"All right." Disappointment tinged her tone, but it was for the best.

Cameron withdrew from her embrace and slipped out the door. He waited until Kristen had locked it behind him to head to the car. Tomorrow couldn't come fast enough.

Chapter Five

"Hey, Kristen, do we have any more scones?" Skye yelled from the front of the café the next morning.

"Ten minutes." Despite the late night, Kristen had been up early and full of energy. The café had been hopping when she made her way down at eight. Skye and Tim had it covered, but the scones were disappearing fast.

It was only ten thirty, and already, she'd baked a dozen strawberry and a dozen blueberry scones. Was the whole town coming into her café today?

She'd resisted going out to check on things. Skye would tell her if she needed help. Plus, she liked being back here in the kitchen. The timer went off, and she pulled another dozen raspberry scones out before putting another dozen plain ones in.

Kristen blew back a piece of hair from her face. What a Saturday, but in a way, it was good that she'd been so busy. It didn't give her time to dwell on what she told Cameron last night. He'd been very good about not asking her about her family, and for that she was grateful. She wanted nothing to do with her parents. They had never really seen her as a person. They never cared for her happiness or well-being. Only her grandmother had.

Lord, she missed her grandmother. She had nursed her grandmother until her death and never regretted a moment of it. Her passing spurred Kristen to be where she was today, to make the changes needed to get away from her toxic parents.

Pushing those thoughts away, she finished boxing up the scones then put the quiches into the oven. They would be done by twelve fifteen. Skye or Tim could box them up for her when they cooled.

Kristen glanced at the clock. It was eleven forty-five. She gnawed at her lower lip. What should she wear today for her date with Cameron?

Cameron had said they were going to talk about wants and needs. Hell, half the time she didn't know what she wanted or needed. She shook her head. Honesty and communication. She could do that. At least, she hoped she could. The only person who had been honest in her life was her grandmother. She hadn't had a lot of honesty or communication in her life. Lord knows her boyfriends had lied. As for her parents, their form of communication was to ignore her. To make a relationship with Cameron, she'd learn to communicate even if it killed her. If she didn't try, she'd regret it the rest of her life.

The oven timer went off, and she called out to Skye, who hurried into the kitchen.

"The scones are done for Mrs. Jenkins; you'll just need to box them up. I've got another three dozen in the fridge. All you'll need to do is bake them if you need them. If not, I'll bake them tomorrow for Monday."

"No problem, go have fun with my brother." Skye turned to leave the kitchen.

"Skye." Kristen waited for her to turn around. It was hard for Kristen to blow off work, even for an afternoon. "Thanks for everything."

"Hey." Skye crossed over and pulled Kristen into her arms. "That's why I'm here. Besides, I love you like a sister."

The bell over the door rang. Skye released her and hurried from the kitchen. Kristen's eyes filled with happy tears. A sister. She'd never had a sister. Or even a best friend.

Blinking away the happy tears, Kristen made her way upstairs to her apartment. What should she wear? She opened her closet door and surveyed the contents.

Cameron had said they were going to his house. Jeans and a shirt would probably be best. Kristen took a quick shower, dressed, and then put her hair into a messy bun. At least it was off her face.

At one on the dot, a knock sounded at her front door. With one last glance in the mirror, she picked up her purse and went to the door.

Cameron stood there in black jeans and a gray T-shirt. The material of both molded to his body, making her mouth water. Hot damn. Talk about sex on two legs. How was it possible that she could be with a man like Cameron?

"Are you finished?" he asked.

"Huh?"

His eyes held laughter as did the grin on his face.

It had been so hard to see him walk away last night after he'd left her apartment. She'd known it was the right thing to do, but she'd bit her lip from calling him back. Cameron stepped closer and drew her into his arms. His lips claimed hers, his tongue thrusting into her mouth.

Oh, hell yeah. She'd dreamt about his kisses last night. Hot, hard, and sensuous. His arms slid around her waist, palms cupping her ass, pulling her against him.

Kristen's fingers gripped his shoulders, holding on for dear life as the kiss went on. Her tongue tangled with his, dueling, tasting, and playing. This was a kiss of a man who knew what he wanted, and she loved every second of it.

Cameron lifted his head.

She drew in a deep breath as she rested her forehead against his chin. "A girl could get used to kisses like that."

"Then I better do it often to keep you addicted."

There was laughter in his voice, and she smiled as she lifted her head. "Ready to go?"

"Yep." Cameron pulled her out the door, barely allowing her to lock up.

"In a hurry?" she asked.

"I want to be alone with you."

Her heart jumped. Part of her whispered that she needed to take this slow, but damn, hadn't she taken it slow enough over the last four years? She'd known Cameron almost as long as she'd known Skye. While she had dated a couple guys here in Grant, she hadn't slept with either of them. It was time to end the drought and explore a relationship with Cameron.

Fifteen minutes later, they pulled up to a large cabin away from the main roadway. As they drove up the private road, she took in the view. The trees were set back and created a "back to nature" look. Cameron helped her out of the car, but she just stood and stared.

"It's beautiful." She gazed at the stunning structure. The house looked rustic with its wooden cabin exterior and modern with large windows and gleaming steel frames. A car port was off to one side.

"Thanks." He took her hand and led her inside.

Kristen stopped, stunned at the way the windows let in the natural light and the high ceiling. Cameron glanced back at her.

"Holy crap," she said.

The door had opened into the main floor with an open floor plan. The sun flowed through the windows into the room. The living room held a sofa, love seat, and two overstuffed chairs. A big-screen TV sat on the mantle above the fireplace, and a multi-colored throw rug covered the hardwood floor.

"Kristen?" He nudged her in the side.

"It's…" She waved her hand. "I love the open floor plan and all the light." She slipped her shoes off before taking a step onto the rich, hardwood floor.

"I had the house built the way I wanted it." He slipped out of his shoes before guiding her into the center of the cabin. "Kitchen and dining room." He waved to where the dark table with four chairs sat. The kitchen was big and roomy with shiny appliances.

"I have an office back there." He gestured toward the partially opened door beyond the staircase. "Upstairs, there are two bedrooms and a loft."

"It feels like you." Kristen didn't know how to explain it. She could picture Cameron in the kitchen, fixing dinner or in his office, grading papers or sitting on the sofa with a beer, cheering on his favorite sports team. The cabin had that homey feeling to it. Nothing like the house she grew up in where she had felt like a visitor.

"Go sit in the living room, and I'll grab us something to drink." He turned her toward the sofa before giving her a swat on her ass.

"Hey," she said but smiled at him.

"My house, my rules."

"We'll see about that." She couldn't keep the laughter from her voice. She was relaxed with Cameron, and she liked it. The pale-brown sofa was buttery soft as she sat down. The fabric something was close to microfiber, soft yet resilient.

"Iced tea," Cameron said, striding into the room with a glass in each hand. He placed them on decorative coasters on the coffee table before sitting down next to her on the sofa.

Kristen curled her legs underneath her and positioned herself so she was facing him.

Cameron cleared his throat. "I know we've discussed certain things already, but I need to know your limits, your wants, your needs."

She nodded nerves danced in her stomach as she leaning over to pick up her tea. She took a sip before setting it back down. "Ask away."

"You mentioned being tied up. Do you like to be restrained?"

"As long as I feel safe, I'm fine with it."

"Any restraint you don't want used?"

Kristen tilted her head. "I'm not sure what you mean."

His lips curved up, and his eyes sparkled with heat. "Scarves, rope, handcuffs, cuffs with rope, spreader bar, things like that."

She shifted her position. Excitement made her skin tingle. How could she be getting turned on already? They were just talking. "All those are fine."

"Have you ever been flogged?"

An excited jolt went through her at his question.

"No." Her voice lowered. "But I'd like to be." She tucked her chin down toward her chest while apprehension warred with eagerness.

"Kristen," he said.

"I…" How could she talk to him about this? Her first boyfriend had never asked her what she wanted, and her ex…Well, he had thought she was a freak.

"Sweetheart." Warm strong fingers slid beneath her chin and lifted it until she gazed into his crystal-blue eyes. "You know what I do for a living?"

"Yes, you teach sexual health at the university."

"Right, I teach the students about sexuality and alternative lifestyles. But I do more than that. I volunteer at Decadence, the BDSM club in town. I also teach education courses there for new members. There's no reason to be embarrassed."

"It's hard for me." She shifted her legs and took a deep breath. He wanted honesty from her, and regardless of her nerves churning in her stomach, she would do this. Gathering her courage she continued, "The men in my life were not very receptive to kink or my kink."

"Then they were idiots." He released her chin. "I'm a Dom. I will always take care of you. Your wants and needs come first. It is my job to take care of you while you're with me."

"But—"

"There are no buts." Cameron turned to her, and Kristen sucked in a breath.

She couldn't explain it, but suddenly he seemed bigger, taller, more…well, dominant.

"Kneel on the floor at my feet."

The command vibrated through her body as Kristen

slid from her position on the sofa to her knees at his feet. Cameron grinned and a shudder went through her. She'd obeyed him without a second thought. Surprise shot through her.

"A true submissive," he whispered.

"But how can I be so submissive?" She gazed up at him, confusion swirling in her brain. "From everything I've read, I have submissive tendencies, but I've never obeyed anyone instantly." She shook her head even as a tremor of need swept up her spine. "I fought to be my own person for a very long time."

"Maybe I should clarify; you're a sexual submissive."

"Explain that to me, please?" Maybe she didn't know as much about BDSM as she thought.

"Sit back on the sofa." He patted the cushion, and Kristen resumed her seat. "You understand Dominant/slave versus the Dominant/submissive?"

"I thought I did. Usually, the Dom/slave is a twenty-four/seven type of relationship where the slave really has no say."

"Depending on the relationship, yes."

Relationship? The word bounced in her brain. She never thought of the Dominant/slave dynamic as a relationship. "Then Dom/submissive just happens at a club or a play party." That's was what she thought. It was for outside the home.

"Not quite." He ran a finger down her arm, causing a delicious tingle of anticipation to flow through her veins. "Sometimes in a D/s relationship, the couple keeps their full-time roles, be it in the home, outside the home, or at a club or party."

Kristen nodded. What did she want? What did

Cameron want? Would their needs match up? Or would she be lacking once again? Her stomach quivered as she waited for him to continue.

"Then, there is a sexual submissive."

"I'm not sure I understand." While she'd read a lot about BDSM, it had been in fiction romance books. She never noticed a distinction even the tutorial websites she'd read. What had she missed in her reading? Well, she'd missed something that was a given.

"A sexual submissive is only submissive when it comes to the bedroom. They lead normal lives, but when it comes to sex and sexual play, they prefer to be submissive."

She mulled his explanation over. It made sense, but they weren't in the bedroom and were only discussing sex. "And by my kneeling, you jumped to me being a sexual submissive?"

"Partly." He grinned at her. "You also don't like when I tell you to do something outside of a sexual situation."

"That's true."

"You are your own woman. You've built up a business, you run the business, and you do a damn good job at it."

"Thank you." She smiled at him. His praise made her feel proud.

"You don't need me or any man telling you how to handle it."

"I'd agree with that." She'd never had such an honest conversation with a man before, and she was enjoying it.

"In a D/s relationship, a submissive might run their own business, but they would almost always ask their

Dom for help in making decisions, in running the business, things like that."

"That's so not me." She'd fight him tooth and nail if he tried to interfere with how she ran Cozy Corners, but somehow, she didn't think he would. He was trying to make a point.

"Correct. You want to give up control when it comes to sex."

"Even though I cornered you and kissed you before you left for Scotland?"

"There's nothing wrong with you taking what you want when I don't seem to be paying attention." He ran his thumb over her lips, and she shivered with excitement. "But now that I know you're interested in me and interested in kink, I will be paying attention. Close attention."

She wasn't sure she liked that "close attention" remark, but she'd deal with it. "So now what?"

"Now we go over likes and dislikes, soft limits, hard limits, and find areas where I might be able to push you a bit." He reached to the table behind him and pulled out a clipboard with a stack of papers attached to it.

"That's a lot of questions." She inclined her head toward the papers in his hand.

"Not all are questions." He shifted on the sofa so he faced her, the clipboard resting on his knee. "Ready?"

"As I'll ever be." Kristen turned so she faced Cameron more. Her stomach turned over. Why did she feel she was about to expose her soul to him?

"Let's talk about limits."

"Sure." She was pretty sure she could do that

55

without betraying her unease. She was woefully inexperienced in this, and she hoped it didn't turn Cameron off.

For the next hour, they discussed her limits, his limits, safewords, and his expectations. By the end of their talk, Kristen was much more relaxed and comfortable. She was going into this with her eyes wide open. A tingle of anticipation slipped through her veins.

Cameron hid a smile when Kristen shifted on the sofa again. This shift was slightly different. Before, she had leaned away as if wary. But now, she was leaning closer, hopefully in eagerness.

Actually, that wasn't a bad sign, but a good one. He couldn't help but remember how Julia had been during this phase. Julia had been a submissive before and was all brass and nails. Cameron preferred Kristen's honesty and shy smiles.

He now had a better idea of what Kristen knew and didn't know. He hadn't taken on a novice in a long time, but anticipation flowed through his blood at being able to teach Kristen, at being able have a romantic relationship with her, and to make her his.

"I really don't know much, do I?" Kristen dipped her head.

His first instinct was to lift her chin, but instead, he slid his arm around her waist and tugged her until she was sitting in his lap. Her green eyes grew wide.

"It will come. We all had to start at the beginning." He was going to enjoy teaching her.

"Now what?" She tried to slip off his lap, but he tightened his grip on her waist.

"First, stop trying to wiggle free. Second, relax, and let me hold you."

A sigh left her lips. "I don't relax very well."

"I've noticed." His lips brushed her cheek. "Put your right arm around my back, and close your eyes." He waited until she did as he said. "Now I want you to rest your head on my shoulder."

"I—"

He placed his fingers against her lips. "No arguments. If you want me to stop, say your safeword." He hoped she didn't say it. They weren't doing much, and she needed to learn to trust him, to relax around him.

Kristen puffed out a breath and put her head on his shoulder, but her body remained stiff, her breathing a little too rapid. He wanted relaxed, not anxious. Cameron shifted his legs wider, cradling her closer to his body. Using his right hand, he began rubbing circles on her back.

He continued caressing her until her breathing became deep and even. "That's it." He kept his voice low while moving his hand up to her neck. Some people became very defensive when someone touched their head and neck area.

A shiver slipped through her when his fingers massaged from beneath her hair to her neck, but she didn't stiffen. *Good.*

"That's it, Kristen," he praised, letting her know he appreciated her efforts. "Rest against me, let me take your burdens away for a while."

A sigh left her lips, and her body became languid against his. He plucked the elastic band holding her hair up and spread his fingers out into her hair, kneading her head softly as his left hand skimmed up and down her left arm.

She giggled. "That tickles."

"What does?" He kept tracing her skin on her forearm with the pad of his finger.

"Your finger. Your skin is rough. I wouldn't have expected that from a professor."

Cameron chuckled. "Just because I teach all day doesn't mean I don't work out."

"That's for sure." Her arm rose, and her fingers trailed down his chest to his abs. "No one has abs like these without working out."

His groin tightened at her touch. "Depends on the work out." He captured her fingers and brought them to his lips. He kissed each digit in turn before gently setting her hand back in her lap.

He continued to caress her skin, just letting her learn she could trust him and his touch. As much as he wanted to jump into the relationship, he'd take his time. There was no reason to rush at this point in time.

Chapter Six

Kristen shut her apartment door behind her after Cameron dropped her off. She glanced at the clock—almost twelve-thirty a.m.—and she leaned against the door, clutching two BDSM books to her chest. What a restful afternoon and evening. He hadn't done much but talk and touch her as he held her all afternoon. They hadn't removed a single piece of clothing, but it still had been sensual. He'd kept the touching light and controlled. But it had still aroused her. She had fully expected Cameron to jump right into sex and the lifestyle with her instead of taking it slow.

He'd somehow known she needed to relax to feel more comfortable with him. Pushing away from the door, she crossed over to the living room, set the two books on the coffee table, and plopped down on her sofa. She had to admit Cameron had been right to take this slow. She wanted to explore Dom/sub relationship with him, but she also wanted a real relationship.

She glanced at the books. He'd given her homework like she was one of his students. Well in a way, she was. But this was going to be an up close and personal study. With a grin, she rose from the sofa and headed for bed. She was a little put off that he didn't try anything today. She so wanted more of his kisses, maybe a caress or two. Her nipples tightened, causing her to take a deep breath as unfulfilled desire sank into her bones. Tomorrow. Tomorrow was another day.

****

"Damn," Kristen swore three days later as she rummaged through the fridge in the café kitchen. "I know darn well it's here."

"Whatcha looking for?" Skye asked as she sauntered into the kitchen.

"Butter." She shifted stuff around in the fridge. Not there. Slamming the door shut, she marched over to the other one. Not there, either. What the hell? Stop. Breathe. Her frustration was over-running her common sense.

"Ummm, Kristen."

Her head shot up. It wasn't like Skye to be tentative about anything. "What happened?"

"It's Tuesday, and I opened today. The delivery never showed up." Skye looked down at her shoes.

Crap. That's why there wasn't any butter.

"It's not your fault." Kristen smiled at Skye to ease her fears. Kristen blamed herself for not being here this morning. Instead of getting up, she'd slept in. Disappointment warred within her. She needed to explain to Cameron that she needed to be home at a decent time when she had to work the next morning. These late nights were causing her to forget about her business, and that was something she couldn't allow to happen. "But I should have told you the second you came downstairs."

"Skye." Kristen crossed over to her and laid her hand on Skye's shoulder. "You were slammed with customers this morning. I'll call and find out what happened. In the meantime, we'll just have to make do with what we have."

The bell over the door rang, and Skye grimaced at being interrupted.

Kristen squeezed Skye's shoulder before dropping her arm and saying, "Really, it's okay. Go take care of the customers."

"Thanks." Skye slid out the kitchen door.

Kristen picked up the phone and called her vendor. "Hey, Pete, Kristen here. My delivery didn't show up this morning."

"Yeah, I know. Sorry," Pete said. "Two of my trucks broke down."

She pushed out a breath. "And you didn't think about calling and letting me know?"

"Look, it's been a little hectic here."

"I'm sorry, Pete. But you have to understand, I rely on your delivery. *Your* on-time delivery. "

"It will be there tomorrow." The line went dead.

Kristen sighed. Damn, it looked like it was time for her to find another supplier, which was not something she wanted to do. She loved using local vendors for her supplies, but if Pete couldn't make his deliveries, she'd find someone who could.

"Skye?" she called to the front. One of them would need to make a run to the warehouse store. She couldn't wait until tomorrow.

"Yeah, boss." Skye looked over the swinging doors into the kitchen. "You want to make a warehouse run, or me?"

Skye glanced over her shoulder, and Cameron peered around Skye, grinning at her. Kristen's eyes widened.

"Why don't we make that run?" Cameron asked.

"W—we?" Kristen could barely get the word out.

Her nerves tingled with the idea of spending more time with him.

"Yes." Cameron slid around his sister and through the doors to where she stood. "I can help you get whatever you need."

"That's a great idea," Skye said. "Cam's got his big SUV with him, and you can pack more into it."

"But…"

Cameron's blue eyes focused in on her, and she forgot what she was going to say.

"Tim will be here in thirty minutes, so he and I can handle the lunchtime rush," Skye said. "We'll be fine."

Cameron ran a finger down her cheek. "I want to help."

"See, all set. Take your time." Skye disappeared from her sight.

"We have to go over to Greenville," Kristen said, hoping he didn't mind.

"Not a problem. Go grab your purse, and let's go."

"Let me find the order invoice first." She started to turn, but Cameron's hands on her shoulders stopped her. Heat filled her blood. His touch was gentle and yet affected her to the core. She was comforted and aroused at the same time. And she wanted more.

"Tell me where the invoice is. I'll grab it." His hands slid from her shoulders, down her arms, until they circled her waist. "Let me help you, Kristen. You don't have to do everything alone."

Her breath caught in her throat at his words. She was so used to doing everything alone. She only had herself to rely on. "I'll get my purse. The invoice should be in the bottom drawer of the cabinet over there. Pete's Supplies." She slid from his arms and ran up the back stairs before she thought better of it.

Kristen high-tailed it up to her apartment and back downstairs. Cameron was bent over going though the files. Damn, the man had a fine ass. Heat filled her face. When was the last time she had ogled a man's ass? Never.

Clearing her throat, she said, "Since we're going, let me check non-perishable supplies." She scooted over to another door.

"Got it," Cameron said.

She picked up the small clipboard and began checking stock.

"Organized little thing, aren't you," he said, standing in the doorway of the supply room.

She threw him a grin over her shoulder. "You have to be in this business. You can't tell me as a professor you're not organized every week when you walk into class."

"That I am."

"Are you sure you don't mind going with me to pick up what I need?" She checked off the items she needed. "I don't want to take up your time."

"I was coming to see if I could convince you to come to lunch with me. I want to spend time with you."

His words warmed Kristen's heart. She turned, and he was right in front of her. Her breath caught in her chest at his nearness. A warm finger traced her cheek. "Are you ready to do some serious shopping?" Those weren't the words she planned on saying, but his touch short-circuited her brain.

He laughed and kissed her cheek. "How bad can it be?"

****

63

Cameron shook his head two hours later. What had he gotten himself into? Kristen had filled a flatbed and an oversized grocery cart with flour, sugar, butter, spices, water, juice, soft drinks and assorted fruits. When the total came up, she didn't even blink. She just ran her bank card.

"I didn't realize how much some of this cost," he said as they pushed the carts toward his SUV. He'd been to the wholesale store before, but he'd bought nothing like this.

"It can get expensive, which is why I buy from local vendors as much as possible. But when a vendor misses a delivery, I have to find an alternative source."

He put the seats down in his SUV so they'd have more room. "I'll do the heavy stuff." He gestured to the bags of flour and sugar.

"Cameron, I lift these all the time." She blew a piece of her brunette hair away from her eyes.

"I know." They'd had a brief argument in the store, but he'd given her a pointed look, and she'd shut her mouth. "But I'm here to help."

"Fine." She waved her hands at the car before crossing her arms over her chest.

Cameron was sweating by the time he finished loading everything into his vehicle. Kristen put the carts back into the corral then jogged over to the passenger side and climbed inside.

He glanced over at her. Her arms were still crossed over her chest. "Are you still annoyed with me?" he asked as they pulled out of the parking slot.

She let out a sigh. "A bit. I'm used to do things on my own."

"I get that, but as your Dom, I'm here to help you

with whatever you need help with. I'm not taking over, Kristen. I'm helping."

"I get it. I don't have to like it, but I get it."

He grinned at her disgruntled words. As he drove to her café, he glanced over at her. Her hands rested in her lap. She fit his vehicle. She wasn't afraid to climb right up into it without help, or without a comment about how high up it was.

"What the hell?" Kristen said as they pulled around the corner. There was a line out the door of her café.

Cameron quickly pulled around back. He'd barely stopped his SUV as she opened the door and jumped out to run inside.

He shook his head and followed after her. The raised voices when he walked in the back door made him wince. He strode to the front of the café, stopped, and stared.

The noise of the line of people snaking through the café was deafening, plus the opened door allowed street noise to enter as well. His sister's hands shook as she tried to work the coffee machine.

Kristen put her fingers into her mouth and whistled.

The room went silent.

"Okay, folks. Sorry, it seems my normal help didn't arrive today. Give me a few minutes to sort things out."

The crowd grumbled but settled down. Skye finished with the coffee and handed it to the waiting customer before turning to Kristen. "I'm sorry," she whispered.

"Nothing to be sorry about." Kristen patted her shoulder. "Where's Tim?"

"His mom fell and broke her hip. I told him I could handle it. And I could have, until half the campus showed up. I forgot it was freshman day."

"No worries."

"What can I do to help?" Cameron was impressed by the exchange between his sister and Kristen. Most owners would be yelling and screaming, but not Kristen. She had handled the situation like a pro.

Kristen looked up at him and smiled. "Okay, here's the game plan. I'll handle the register and orders. Cameron, you get the food orders. Skye, do coffee orders."

"You got it, boss." Cameron gave her a salute.

"I'll get Cam an apron." Skye scurried into the kitchen.

"Do I really need one?" Cameron asked.

"Yep. Besides, you'll look cute."

Skye returned with the apron.

Cameron took it from her and slipped it on. "What do I do?" he asked.

"I'll tell you what food the customer wants," Kristen said. "Just use the tongs. If the order is for here, use a plate, which are stacked on the shelf to your right. If it's to go, the bags are on your left."

He glanced up at the crowd. "Let's do this," he whispered, dropping a kiss on Kristen's cheek. He could handle this.

"We're ready," Kristen said as she began taking orders.

Three hours later, Cameron leaned against the counter, more tired than if he'd been teaching all day and then spent the evening at the club. The café was fairly quiet now with just a few people sitting at tables.

He marveled at Kristen and his sister. They'd finally worked through the entire crowd plus the others who'd shown up.

"Remind me to tell Mom and Dad how hard you work," he said to Skye.

"Thought this was all fun and games, huh, big brother." Skye bumped his hip.

"Is it always like that?" he asked.

"Lunchtime can be a little hectic." Kristen leaned against the counter. "But as the kids come back onto campus, it's crazy, especially on freshman day. I can't believe I forgot about it."

"Now what?" Cameron studied Kristen. Some of her brunette hair had escaped the confines of her pony tail and brushed her face. Her eyes were bright, and she had a smile on her face.

"Oh my God, the food." She slapped her forehead. "It's still in the SUV."

"Easy." His hand descended on her shoulders. "Remember that quick break I took a while ago? I got all the perishables and put them in the fridge."

"You're great." She brushed a kiss over his cheek. "Can I hire you?"

"One job at a time," he whispered in her ear. "My first job is teaching you about kink. My second is convincing you to have a relationship with me."

Kristen's eyes widened, and he grinned.

"Okay you two, no foreplay at work," Skye said.

"And what would you know about foreplay?" Cameron frowned at his sister.

"Don't ask, don't tell," Kristen piped up, nudging Cameron toward the kitchen. "Skye, if you'll do a quick inventory, we'll finish getting the stuff out of the

SUV."

"You got it."

"But—" Cameron started to protest. He wanted to grill his sister for more details. She was his baby sister, and he didn't want to see her hurt.

"In the kitchen, big boy." Kristen pushed him in the back until she had him in the kitchen.

"Kristen." He turned to face her once he found himself halfway through the kitchen.

She held up her hand as she stepped through the doorway. "I know she's your sister, Cameron, but there are certain things you don't ask your baby sister. Period."

"I'm her older brother. I want to know who she's seeing." He crossed his arms over his chest.

"Really?" She sauntered closer to him. "Do you really want Skye to know how kinky we are?"

He sobered. "That's different."

Kristen laughed. "How? Because she's a woman."

"No, she's my sister."

"So that means you are going to tell her how kinky we are?"

Cameron shook his head. When had he lost control of the situation? "What's between us is between us. It's no one else's business."

She poked him in the chest. "And the same goes for Skye's love life. You may be her big brother, but if she wants you to know, she'll tell you. She has a right to her privacy."

"Yes, but…" He sputtered as Kristen marched to the back door and opened it. Damn it, Kristen was right, but he didn't have to like it.

"Now, let's get that stuff unloaded." She grinned at

him. "I love watching the way your muscles bulge as you lift things."

The mischief in her green eyes made him smile. She'd gone from resenting his help to accepting it. He was making progress.

****

Later that evening, Cameron sat in the café kitchen, enjoying the fresh baked smell of raspberry tarts as he reviewed his class schedule while Kristen baked.

"How often do you have to run out and get your own supplies?" he asked.

"Not often." She slid another pan of goodies into the oven before striding over to him.

"That's a good thing." He snagged her around her waist and pulled her onto his lap.

"Yes." She let out a sigh and relaxed against him. "What a day."

"It was busy. I'm happy we're able to spend time together tonight." After the crisis in the café today, he had figured their night together would be delayed.

"Me, too." She started to sit up.

"Stay here," he ordered.

She relaxed against his body, her head resting on his shoulder. "You were a trooper today, thanks for all the help."

"You're welcome." His lips brushed her temple. "Have you thought about hiring more help?"

"Yes. But most of my help comes from the university, so I have to work around their class schedule."

"What about someone to bake for you?" To him, that would make logical sense if she couldn't hire more help for the café.

She shook her head. "That's my baby. It's relaxing, unless I've had a day like today." She smothered a yawn.

"How often do you have days like this?" Cameron ran his hand over her back, gently caressing her muscles. She'd worked hard today. They all had, but he'd found some satisfaction in helping her.

"Not often, thank goodness. We usually just have steady business in the mornings from seven until about nine, then again from eleven until two."

"But you stay open until six."

"Yes, but when school resumes, we have a stream of customers from the university from two until four."

"So close at four." He was aware that a small business owner like Kristen needed to make money by being open when the customers wanted. But what drove her to do almost everything herself and keep such long hours?

She shook her head. "People stop by on their way home from work to pick up treats, and that's usually when we figure out what needs to be baked for the next day, what we ran short of, check on supplies, all that other fun stuff."

"I'm going to get nosy here. Who takes care of your books?" How much was she taking on herself?

"I do."

"Why not hire someone?" He needed to understand her need for control.

She squirmed on his lap. "I'm not good at letting things go, Cameron."

"I've noticed." He chuckled. "But you let me help today." Skye had convinced Kristen to let him help her with the shopping, and as for working in the café... He grinned. Kristen had ordered him to help, not that it bothered him. He kind of liked that side of her.

"It was crisis mode. All hands on deck when the ship is starting to sink." The timer beeped, and she slipped off his lap. "That's it. I'm done for tonight."

He glanced at the clock. It was only eight-thirty, but he had an early meeting with the dean tomorrow.

Kristen put the goodies away then turned to him. "What's on the agenda for tonight?"

"Bed." He grinned when her eyes widened. "You in your bed and me in mine." Though he really wanted to explore with her more, he'd wait until she wasn't exhausted.

"Tease."

He laughed. "Come on. I'll walk you up to your place."

"It's just upstairs."

"Humor me." He snagged her around the waist and led her over to the stairs, double checking to make sure the back door was locked before guiding her up to her apartment. Her feet dragged, and part of him was glad he had an early morning meeting.

"Lock the door after me and then go to bed."

"Bossy," she said then yawned.

"Just remember that." He gave her a light kiss before opening the door. "Just wait until Saturday."

Her eyes widened. "What is Saturday?"

"If I told you, it wouldn't be a surprise." He slipped out the door and waited on the landing until he heard the dead bolt being thrown. Saturday. Plans already ran through his mind.

Chapter Seven

Kristen pulled the spinach cups out of the oven and slid in a pan of cheesy bacon cups. She'd been wanting to try these recipes, and since she was up early for a Saturday morning, she figured it was a good time. She was excited about Cameron's plans for the day. Since the crazy day on Wednesday, they hadn't spent much time together. Thursday, Cameron had had a meeting at the university, and when he'd stopped by the café afterward, she had seen the lines of tiredness around his eyes.

And last night... Her lips turned up. She'd promised Skye the day off, so she was almost asleep on her feet when he'd stopped by as she was closing. He'd kissed her then told her to get some rest before escorting her up to her apartment and leaving.

The bell on the café door rang, and Kristen moved over to the entrance between the kitchen and front counter. Skye came bouncing in, locking the door behind her.

Turning, Skye let out a squeal. "Kristen, you scared me."

"Sorry." She pushed open the swinging door for Skye. "I was up early and decided to try out a couple of new recipes."

"Excited?"

What did Skye know that she didn't? "About

what?" Kristen moved the now-cooled spinach cups off the baking sheet, putting four on a plate before sliding the rest into the fridge.

"Spending the day with Cameron, of course."

"Is there anything you don't know?" Kristen put her hands on her hips. She hadn't mentioned her date to Skye.

"No." After putting her purse and jacket away, Skye slid her apron on. "Besides, I think it's great you're seeing him. You two have...what is the word? Chemistry."

Kristen ducked her head. Damn, what else was Skye seeing? What were other people seeing? Did they see her excitement, her desire? Would they judge her because of it? A bubble of unease slid up her spine. Was this relationship a good idea? "I didn't realize it was that obvious."

"Only to me."

Kristen gave a sigh of relief. Skye's words calmed her nerves over being with Cameron...at least for now.

Skye sauntered over and stared down at the food. "Mmm, those look good."

"Try it, and give me your opinion."

Skye snatched one of the spinach cups and popped it into her mouth. Her eyes grew wide.

"That bad?" Kristen asked.

Skye shook her head. "Oh my God," she said once she swallowed. "Those are great. What are they?" She picked up another one and ate it.

"Spinach, garlic, sour cream, cream cheese, and grated cheese mixed together, then put in a pastry puff and baked." The oven timer went off, and Kristen pulled the bacon cheddar cups out.

"Bacon." Skye grinned. "These are going to be a big hit."

"I hope so." She playfully slapped Skye's hand as she reached for one of the bacon cups. "Let them cool."

"Are we putting them out today?"

"Yes, provided you don't eat them all."

Skye picked up a bacon cup and blew on it before taking a bite. "Dang, Kristen. I don't know how you come up with these things."

Kristen shook her head. "I saw the pastry cups the other day and bought them, and then wondered what I could fill them with. Breakfast for most of the kids at the university is on the run, and these are small enough."

"Plus great for parties," Skye said before she glanced at the clock. "Five to eight, I'll get the coffee going and then open."

"Thanks, Skye."

With a wave, Skye went out to the café, and Kristen began making more of the pastry cups. They could sit in the fridge, and Skye could bake them if she needed. Now, she could experiment on a new cake recipe.

"Hey, it's almost eleven," Skye said, popping her head into the kitchen.

"What?" Kristen almost dropped the pan she was holding. It couldn't be. She'd just looked at the clock a few minutes ago, and it had said nine forty-five.

"Wasn't Cameron picking you up at eleven?"

"Crap." She glanced at the clock. Ten fifty. She sat the pan down and took off her oven mitts. "Time got away from me."

"Go. Tim's already here."

"Okay, if you need anything…"

"Yeah, I'll call. Go." Skye made a shooing motion with her hands.

Kristen jogged up the stairs to her apartment. Thank goodness, she had laid out clean clothes. Now, she needed a quick shower. As she dried herself off, she heard a loud knock on the door. She wrapped the towel around her and padded to the door. Looking out the peephole, she saw Cameron standing there with a frown on his face.

She fumbled with the locks before pulling the door open. "Sorry, time got away from me." When Cameron didn't say anything, she glanced up at him.

The frown was gone, and his gaze blazed with desire. He stepped forward, causing her to retreat. Once inside he slammed the door.

"Drop the towel."

"What?" Her heart raced. He had this…she didn't know what to call it other than, his Dom look. His eyes were dark with desire, he looked bigger, more muscular… Her bones just about melted.

"Drop. The. Towel."

Oh God, *that voice*. The deep, husky, commanding tone went straight to her core, making her wet. Her fingers trembled as she loosened the towel from around her chest. Was she really going to do this? Was she ready to do this?

Cameron's warm fingers closed over hers. "Am I moving too fast?"

She wanted to deny it, but…what? He was going to see her naked somewhere along the line. "No, I just didn't expect you to demand me to drop my towel." Hadn't she complained to herself the other day that he was moving too slow?

"Ground rules, remember?" he asked. "When we're alone, I'm in control."

"And I agreed." She blew out a breath as he dropped his hand. Closing her eyes, she loosened the towel and let it fall to the floor. Would he find the flaws that others had?

The silence in the room caused her to shiver with apprehension.

"You are gorgeous." His words were quiet. "Open your eyes, sweetheart."

Kristen raised her chin and let her lashes lift. The look of amazement and wonder on Cameron's face almost brought her to her knees. "You don't mind?" Her voice was soft.

"Mind what?" His fingertips traced her shoulders.

"My breasts are a little small, and my hips a little big."

"They're perfect." His breath brushed her cheek. "You're perfect."

The fabric of his shirt rubbed against her breasts as he moved closer, making her nipples harden as he pulled her into his embrace.

"But..."

"Perfect." His arms tightened around her as his hands cupped her ass. "Don't you believe anyone who tells you anything else." He slapped her ass.

"Cameron." His name came out more excited than startled.

"As much as I'd like to keep you this way, I do have plans for today. So go get dressed." He stepped back.

She missed his warmth and touch, but with a saucy

grin, she turned and sashayed her way to her bedroom.

Cameron adjusted his cock in his jeans. Damn, seeing her dressed in just a towel had made him harden, but then when she'd dropped it...full-on erection. He strode over to the window and looked out at the street.

He needed to calm his dick down. Otherwise, today's plans would go up in smoke. It was the end of their first week together. They'd spent time doing what normal couples did. Cameron let out a laugh.

Normal couples. Kink was perfectly normal. But he hadn't rushed the kinky stuff. Instead, he'd taken her out to dinner and had spent time with her while she baked. They'd kissed, but today, he was going to up the ante. He would show her his playroom and see how she reacted.

After seeing her perfect body, he wanted nothing more than to take her to bed. Maybe tonight. No. Not yet. They could play. He wanted to learn her body, hear her cries of pleasure, and read every nuance she had before they moved on to more relationship stuff.

"Ready," she said.

He turned. She was dressed in a pair of jeans with a flowered T-shirt and sneakers.

"Great." He held his hand out to her, pleased when she slipped hers into his.

Kristen locked the door when they stood on the landing, and he kept her hand in his as they negotiate the stairs down to his car. He was reluctant to let go of her as he held the car door open for her. She climbed in and once he made sure she was in, he let go. Cameron rounded the car and climbed in.

"What's on the agenda for today?" Kristen asked as he pulled away from the café.

"It's a surprise." He tossed her a grin. "Did you finish reading the book I gave you?"

"Yes. Oh darn, I left it in my bedroom."

"I don't need it back; you keep it." He turned onto the road leading out of town. He'd given her a book on the D/s lifestyle and what it could contain. "So what did you think?"

"Interesting."

"More than that, Kristen. Was there anything in the book you didn't understand? Anything that you are worried about?" He was happy she found it interesting, but he wanted to answer any questions she might have.

She wiggled in her seat. "Nothing I can think of. It seemed pretty basic."

He nodded as he turned into his driveway. "Good." He parked, and together, they strode up the walk and into his house. After removing their shoes at the door, he guided her to the family room and motioned toward the forest green sofa. "Have a seat."

He waited until they both sat before he started speaking. "I want to go over a few rules before we do anything today."

"Okay." She twisted a lock of hair around her finger.

Damn, he wasn't trying to make her nervous, but he wanted to make sure she understood she could call a halt to anything at any time.

"I want you to talk to me, ask me anything you need to ask. There is nothing off limits with us anymore." He waited for her to respond.

Her gaze darted around the room as if she was trying to come up with an answer. "But my hard limits?"

"Hard limits are still in effect. But if you have questions about something I'm doing—want to know about a toy, have a concern, anything at all—I want you to talk to me. I don't want you scared or frightened."

Her lips turned up in a grin. "I think some fear is natural."

"Maybe, but I don't want you running away." It would crush his heart if he frightened her away.

"Not going to happen."

"Good. What is your safeword?"

"Bacon."

"To get me to slow down?"

"Cheese."

He smiled; she had told him she used food as safewords because it was something she would remember but wouldn't use during playtime by accident.

"All right. I want to make sure you're okay with what is going to happen today."

"Cameron." She placed her hand on his arm. "I'm fine with you. Otherwise I wouldn't be here."

"Negotiation. I'm not going to tell you everything." If for some reason things didn't work out between then, he wanted her to be able to negotiate with others. His gut tightened. Just the thought of her with someone else made him sick.

"All right."

"Today, we're going to be in my playroom."

"You have a playroom?" There was eagerness in her voice, and it pleased him.

"Yes. We're going to explore it together today. And probably try a few things out."

Her eyes lit up, and his own excitement rose.

"What are we waiting for?"

He laughed. "Eager little thing, but first things first." He dipped his head and captured her lips with his. Subtle hints of coffee and raspberries teased his taste buds as they kissed.

She followed his lips as he pulled back from the kiss, and he fought against hauling her against him. One thing at a time.

"So here's how we're going to proceed today." His fingers brushed down her cheek. "You're going to look around my playroom. Note anything that is a hard limit that we haven't already discussed."

"What do you have in there?"

"You'll see. After that, I'd like to see how you respond to being tied up on the equipment of my choice."

"That's fine." Her eyes were bright with excitement.

Cameron took her hand, stood, and guided her down the hall, coming to a stop in front of a closed, oak door. "Open the door and go in, the lights are already on." He released her hand.

She had to take this step herself. It had to be her choice, not his, to explore his lifestyle.

Chapter Eight

Kristen placed her fingers around the door handle as Cameron stepped back from her in the hallway outside his playroom. Her heart pounded. Was she really going to do this? Oh, hell yeah. She was dying to see his playroom. She pushed the handle down, and the door slid open.

Her breath caught in her throat. The room was decorated in deep reds, browns, and black. Various pieces of equipment were spread around the room, cabinets set off to one side. She tried to take it all in.

"If there's anything you want to know more about, or an explanation about, let me know."

"This is all yours?"

"Yes. I've been collecting for a long time."

Kristen stepped into the room. The floor under her feet was different. It looked like hardwood when she glanced down but didn't have the hardwood feel to it. "The floor is different."

"A special type of tile that matches the hardwood, but it's softer and easier to clean."

She nodded and walked over to the row of open cabinets. The wood of the cabinets gleamed as if they'd just been polished. The first one held drawers. She opened them one at a time.

Dildos, vibrators, an assortment of insertable toys, and clamps. He probably had a full adult store's worth of items in here. A grin played around her lips when she noticed the cock rings; she wondered if she could convince him to wear one.

The next cabinet held rope, scarves, and cuffs. The last one...her breath whooshed out of her. Several spreader bars and a multitude of floggers and whips hung inside. All different sorts. Different textures and lengths.

But there was also a drawer in the cabinet, and she pulled it open. Kristen tilted her head. These were different, and she wasn't sure what they were. They looked like canes, but not. "What are these?" She gestured to the brightly colored items.

"Those are acrylic canes."

"Acrylic?" Her hand rose. "May I touch them?"

"Yes."

Kristen ran her fingers over the bright-blue colored one. There were several colors and sizes. There were a couple of clear ones, one that looked like a big square, and another made into a spiral. "And these?" She pointed to a set of small ones that actually looked like fiber optic cables.

"Ah, those." Cameron reached around her and picked one up. "These are for more delicate areas, to tease you with." He tapped one against her breast over her clothing.

Heat burst over her skin. "Okay." Her voice was a little high, but pure passion flowed over her skin at the thought of Cameron using them on her delicate parts.

She turned from the cabinets to observe the rest of the room. A St. Andrews cross, a spanking bench, a massage table and a longer, bigger spanking bench. There were rings in the ceiling and walls. A swing hung in another corner.

Kristin pivoted on her heel and stared at Cameron. "Now what?"

"No questions?" He tilted his head.

"Nope. Most of the equipment I've seen before. The toys are toys. I'm good."

"Okay. We've never talked about protocols."

She frowned. "Protocols?"

"Yes, I'm not very strict. I know many in the community that are. My main request is when we're at the club or in the playroom, you will call me Sir."

"Yes, Sir." The title flowed from her. Cameron was so different from her first boyfriend, and from those she'd seen in the community. All they had seemed to care about was their own pleasure and humiliating other people.

"Very good. Here's your first test. I want you to undress and lay down on the massage table."

Kristen swallowed as Cameron stared at her. Her heart rate picked up, and her fingers trembled as she slipped off her T-shirt and folded it. Her jeans went next.

"You can put them on the chair." Cameron pointed to a straight-backed chair she hadn't noticed earlier.

Padding to the chair, she set her clothes on the seat then leaned down to slip off her socks. Her back was to Cameron, but he didn't say anything. Now she was just in her bra and panties.

A tremor went through her body. Her bra came off next. Her nipples were already hard and begging for attention. She blew out a breath and slipped her panties off. He'd already seen her naked, so why did this feel different?

Without looking at him, she strode across the room to the massage table and lay down on her back. Her chest rose and fell with her rapid breath. She closed her eyes, trying to find a way to calm herself while she waited for Cameron.

Her ears picked up the rustling of clothing. Then feet padding against the floor. The sound of drawers opening and closing made her shiver. What was he planning?

"You are so beautiful." His breath brushed over her cheeks.

She'd been so lost in thought she hadn't heard him approach her.

"Open your eyes, sweetheart."

Kristen did as he asked.

Cameron was leaning over her, his blue eyes focused on her face. "That was hard for you?"

"Yes, Sir" she whispered.

"Why?"

She wrinkled her nose. "I'm not sure. I mean we've kissed, we've been out together. Hell, you've seen me naked already. This felt different, Sir."

"Tell me what felt different to you?"

Kristen stared into his blue eyes. They were calm, but a flash of desire showed. "Maybe because we're in your playroom. Maybe because this is the first time in a long time I've been naked with a man with the intent of doing something naughty, Sir."

His eyebrows rose. "Are you afraid?"

She shook her head. "Nervous. Excited. But not afraid, Sir."

"Good." He straightened up. "I've got a set of scarves in my hands. I'm going to restrain you."

"Yes, Sir."

He grinned, and warmth filled Kristen's body. She had pleased him. Wait a second. Was she worried about pleasing him?

"Lift your arms over your head and cross your wrists."

She did, and almost immediately, soft, silky fabric slid over her wrists. A shiver danced over her skin. Round and round the fabric went around her wrists until he tied it off.

"Okay?" Cameron's face appeared again. "Not too tight?"

Kristen tugged. There was a little give. "It's fine, Sir."

"Your body is flushed. Are you enjoying this?"

"Yes, Sir."

The pads of his fingers trailed over her sensitive skin from neck, between her breasts, over her belly, then on to her right leg. Cameron's strong fingers encircled her ankle and pulled her legs apart. Kristen stiffened.

"Baby, relax." His grip loosened.

"Sorry, Sir." She tried to command her muscles to release, but nothing happened. Fear had her in its grips. Oh Lord, she couldn't do this. She couldn't let go enough for Cameron to tie her up. She was a failure. Just as her boyfriends had told her. Tears filled her eyes.

"Kristen." Cameron's voice was gentle. His fingers left her ankle and moved to her cheek, stroking it softly.

"I'm sorry," she whispered as a tear slipped from the corner of her eye.

Cameron swore silently. He picked up the safety

scissors, slipped them between her bound wrists and cut the scarf away. The second her hands were free, he dropped the scissors and scooped her into his arms. His warmth surrounded her.

"I've pushed you too fast," he whispered against her hair as he crossed the room and picked up a folded blanket. He strode over to the sofa against the wall.

He sat down and gently cradled her against his body until he maneuvered the blanket around her, and then he put her on his lap. She couldn't seem to stop trembling.

Cameron fought the anger welling in him, anger with himself. "I'm so sorry," he whispered.

Where had he gone wrong? Her body had been flushed with excitement, her breathing a little fast, but nothing that had indicated distress.

"It's not your fault." She sniffled.

Cameron snagged a box of tissues he kept close by. He pulled several out and slipped them into her hand. She dabbed at her eyes and blew her nose.

He held her, going over everything in his head. What had he missed? If he could put his finger on it, maybe he could figure out what scared her.

"Cameron." Her soft fingers touched his cheek. "You did nothing wrong."

He gazed down at her. Her green eyes were bright but clear. She'd stopped shaking and was resting against him, her body lax in his embrace. Her left hand still rested on his cheek, grounding him.

"It is my responsibility to make sure you were ready. I pushed." He berated himself. They needed more time to get to know each other. A week wasn't enough.

"You didn't." She wiggled in his lap. "I just haven't been restrained since that first time. I didn't realize I needed more time to adjust."

"I should have realized it."

"Stop it."

His head jerked up. "What did you say?" Women didn't talk to him like that, especially not in his playroom.

"At least I got your attention, Sir." Her lips curled up. "Please stop blaming yourself. I want to be with you, Cameron. I want to explore kink with you. Neither of us could have predicted what had happened."

"Do you know why you froze up on me?"

"My gut says fear. Not of you, but of old fears." She shivered.

"You're cold." He made a note to make sure to turn the heat up in the playroom the next time they used it.

"A bit." She snuggled into the blanket.

"Let's fix that." He set her on the sofa then stood and crossed the room. He picked her clothes off the chair and brought them to her. "Get dressed. I'll be in the kitchen, making some coffee."

Cameron strode into his kitchen, calling himself all sorts of names. No matter what she said, he was the dominant, and he took his responsibilities seriously. By the time he had two cups of coffee ready, Kristen came in and sat on one of the breakfast bar stools.

"Thanks," she said when he pushed a mug in front of her. She lifted it and sipped then let out a groan. "Hell, you really do pay attention. My coffee is perfect."

He grinned. "Yes, I do." He sipped his own brew then put the cup down. "We need to discuss this."

She sighed. "Do we have to?"

"Open, honest communication. Remember?"

"Damn Dom," she whispered. Her tone was playful, and her body language suggested she was relaxed and calm.

Cameron smiled at her.

"I just froze up," she said in a rush.

"You seem to think I wasn't moving too fast."

"You weren't. I honestly don't know why I froze up. I tried to relax, but I couldn't. Something held me back."

"You mentioned old fears. Any ideas?"

"Maybe it's because of what happened the time I was tied up, and someone took pictures." She shrugged her shoulders. "Is this going to ruin things for us?" She tucked her chin against her chest.

"Absolutely not." He reached over the breakfast bar, and using two fingers, he lifted her chin. "I still want to explore this with you."

"And I with you."

"Then we will. For now, finish up your coffee, and we'll go for a walk."

"Sounds good, but…"

"What is it?"

"Don't you think you should put a shirt on before we go outside?" Laughter lit her eyes.

"Yes, smart ass." He tapped her on the nose with his fingers before going in search of his shirt.

****

Later that evening after having pizza delivered, they curled up on the sofa, watching a science fiction movie. Cameron glanced down to see Kristen had fallen asleep in his arms.

He wasn't surprised. She'd told him she'd been up since four that morning. She really did need help baking, but he'd keep that comment to himself.

What had happened earlier in the playroom still grated on his nerves, but he was glad Kristen trusted him enough to relax and sleep in his embrace. Kristen's reaction to being tied up had lulled him into a sense of compliancy. She'd been so open and excited about everything up until the end.

He ran his schedule through his head, trying to figure out how much time they could have together in the next week. Because he wanted to spend more time with her, to wipe out any worries about what had happened today. His classes started on Wednesday, and he had most of his semester curriculum already done. A plan began to form for the week. He shifted on the sofa, putting both of them into a more comfortable position while he plotted.

****

Kristen didn't want to wake up. She was warm and cozy. She shifted her hand, trying to find her pillow. Instead, she found...her eyes popped open. Cameron? She was touching his stubbled face. But not only that, she was lying on top of him.

The last thing she remembered was the campy science fiction film they were watching on TV, then nothing. She'd fallen asleep on him. How embarrassing. She lifted her head.

How was she going to get out of this? She was wedged between him and the back of the sofa.

"I can hear you thinking; go back to sleep," Cameron muttered.

"I need to get home." She started to push herself

up.

"No, you don't." His arms tightened around her. "Still sleepy."

Kristen sighed as he let out a snore. She had no idea what time it was. The room was dark except for the flickering of the TV screen. How long had she'd been asleep? With a sigh, she laid her head on his chest.

This was nice, Cameron cradling her against his body. She could hear his heart beating and the rhythm of his breathing. A sense of peace invaded her body. She was becoming comfortable with Cameron, and a relationship with him no longer scared her. Maybe she was finally getting over her past.

Chapter Nine

"Should we wake them?"

"Mom is going to have a field day."

Male voices penetrated Kristen's sleep-fogged brain.

"They do make a good couple."

She started to smile...she was still in Cameron's arms from last night. Kristen opened her eyes and saw two of his brothers standing in front of the coffee table, staring at them.

"Ah... Hi, this isn't what it looks like." She pushed against Cameron's chest. "Cameron, wake up." She fought against panicking.

"He can be a pretty deep sleeper," Graham said, his dark blue eyes twinkling and a wide grin on his face. He was the second to the youngest.

"I'll wake him." Alec gave a loud whistle.

"What the hell." Cameron jerked awake, and his arms tightened around her.

"Good morning, brother." The two chorused.

"Oh, crap," Cameron muttered.

"Good thing it was us and not Mom." Graham gave her a wink.

She pushed against Cameron again. "I need to get up," she whispered.

"Go away, you two. Can't you see I'm busy?" Cameron nuzzled her neck.

"Cameron!" She wiggled in his embrace.

"All right." Cameron shifted.

Kristen scrambled to her feet. She stared at his brothers, her face growing warm. "Ah, excuse me." She ran for the bathroom and slammed the door behind her.

Cameron's gaze followed Kristen as she ran down the hallway. Poor thing, she wasn't used to his crazy family.

Alec chuckled. "She'll need to toughen up a bit to be around us, brother."

"Yeah." Cameron ran a hand through his hair. "What are you two doing here?"

"You didn't show up for Sunday breakfast," Graham said.

"So we volunteered to come and fetch you," Alec said. "Who knew you'd be busy with the delectable café owner."

"Back off." Cameron surged to his feet.

"Easy." Alec put his hands up.

"If you two are through, tell Mom I'm sorry, but I won't be having breakfast this morning."

"Oh." Alec's eyebrows rose. "And what do I tell her?"

"Tell her I'm helping Kristen today, and I'm treating her to breakfast. Now shoo." Cameron waved his arms. "You've embarrassed my lady quite enough."

"Your lady?" Graham's eyes lit up with mischief. "Oh how the mighty have fallen."

"Just go."

His brothers' laughter lingered as they closed the front door. Cameron took a deep breath then marched over to the bathroom door.

"Kristen." He knocked. "They're gone."

"I'm so embarrassed." Her faint words barely carried past the door.

"There's no need." He braced his arm against the door frame. He wouldn't test to see if she locked the door. He wanted her to come out on her own.

"But they saw us together."

"Honey, they're going to see a lot more of us together."

"What?" The door opened. Kristen's cheeks were pink.

"If we're going to be seeing each other, the whole town is going to know we're together."

She groaned. "I really didn't think this through."

"Is people seeing us together a problem?" He didn't like that she wanted to keep their relationship quiet.

"Yes and no." She pushed past him. "I need coffee."

Cameron followed her into his kitchen, satisfaction hitting him in the gut at how good she looked there. She opened several cabinets before finding the coffee and filters and pulling them out. She was making herself at home. "Want to explain the 'yes and no'?" He pulled two mugs from the cabinet as she filled the coffee maker with water.

"No, it's not a problem people know we're together, but also yes, there is a problem." She scooped the coffee into the filter and turned it on. "Some people won't approve." She crossed to the fridge and grabbed the creamer.

"Who cares?" He frowned. "It's no one's business but ours." He watched her pace around the kitchen as the coffee percolated.

"Except you don't run a public business." The coffee gave a gurgle and finished. She filled a mug and handed it to him after putting in just a splash of milk.

"I'm missing something." He wasn't sure he followed her train of thought.

"It's like the pastry school all over again. People aren't going to like what we're doing together, and there will be repercussions to my business."

"Sweetheart."

"Cameron, I'm afraid people will stop coming to the café. I'll lose my business, my home, and my dream fails. I can't live through losing my dreams again."

He set his mug down before cupping her cheeks between his palms. "We're consenting adults. If someone stops coming to your café because we're seeing each other, then they aren't people you want to have in your place of business."

"You don't understand." Her eyes dulled.

He took her cup from her hands and set it on the counter before slipping his arms around her waist. "Why don't you explain it to me?"

"Appearances are everything." She let out a sigh.

Her past was making her leery. He did understand. "Let me ask you a question. Do you think any less of me knowing I'm into kink?"

"Of course not."

"Then why do you think people will think less of you for dating me?"

"But we'll be doing more than just dating."

"Sweetheart, half the town sleeps with the other half. No one should look down on you for your private life, and if they do, then that's their problem." He watched her eyes brighten and wondered why she needed such reassurances.

"What about the kink?"

"What about it?" He leaned down and brushed a kiss across her lips. "What's between us behind closed doors is no one's business but ours."

She let out another sigh, but her muscles relaxed, and she leaned against him. "I guess I'm worrying for nothing."

"Not for nothing." He wouldn't belittle her concerns. "Your past has shaped you into what you are today."

"That's not reassuring." She gave a little laugh and pushed away from him.

It pleased him to see her smiling. Their road ahead wasn't going to be smooth, but if they talked things out, it wouldn't be so rocky. "You are a beautiful, talented woman, and don't let anyone tell you otherwise." He picked his mug up and took a fortifying drink.

"Flatterer."

He grinned. "So, how do you feel about trying the playroom again? No restraints this time."

Kristen's hands fluttered to her chest before she grabbed her coffee off the counter and cradled it in her hands. "You won't tie me up?"

"No. You were uncomfortable with it, so we'll take it one step at a time. Today, I'd like to explore your body more and see how you react to my touch and also to my toys."

"Toys?" Her voice went up an octave, but her cheeks flushed with desire.

"Before we do that, we both need to eat, and then, we'll go play." Cameron strode over to the fridge and opened it. He pulled out a box and set it on the counter.

"And when did you pick up breakfast from the café?"

"The advantage of having a sister who works there." He pulled down two plates from the cabinet then opened the box. "Let's see here. Two blueberry scones…those are mine. Oh, this looks like some sort of quiche."

"Mine." She snatched the plate off the counter the second he put the slice of quiche on it. "Ham and spinach quiche. Skye must have snuck a piece away yesterday when I wasn't looking."

"That she did." Cameron grinned. He was happy to see Kristen relaxed and playful. "Heat it up in the microwave so we can eat."

"Yes, boss."

"Not yet, but soon."

Cameron watched Kristen closely as they entered the playroom thirty minutes later. Her eyes were bright with excitement, and her skin flushed. He surveyed the room, trying to decide where he wanted her since restraining her was out of the question.

"Undress," he ordered as he crossed over to the toy cabinets.

He opened the first one, grabbed a vibrator, vibrating egg, and harness before shutting the drawer and opening another one. He grabbed a feather tickler and a small rabbit flogger. Those would all be good for today. He carried the items over to the small table next to one of his flogging benches.

Cameron checked on Kristen, who stood silently next to the chair where she'd put her clothes. "Come over here," he said, motioning to her.

Her gaze bounced between him and the bench as

she walked over to him. "How is this going to work, Sir?" she asked.

"The restrains will remain undone." He undid the Velcro restraints, allowing the ends to hang loose. "Come, climb on." He patted the leather.

Kristen let out a breath and went to the end of the bench. Cameron cupped her chin and turned her face to his. The excitement still shone in her eyes, but her muscles were stiff. "Talk to me. Are you afraid?"

"No, Sir." Her lips twitched. "Not afraid, just unsure how to get onto the bench."

"Ah." He hadn't thought about that, although he should have. She wasn't used to the different dungeon equipment. "I can help you with that." He maneuvered her until she was facing the bench and placed his hands on her waist. "This is a split spanking bench. Your knees go on the lower portion, then you lay down on your stomach with arms on the upper arm rests. You can rest your head in the donut just like a massage table."

She let out a laugh. "No massage table I've ever seen looks like this, Sir."

"Ready?"

Kristen nodded, and he lifted her up. She placed her knees on the rests, and he kept his hands on her waist until she lay on the bench.

"Okay?" he asked, making minor adjustments to her legs and arms.

"Good, Sir." Her reply was muffled. "I feel very exposed, Sir."

"I can imagine." He loved this split bench. It allowed for a sub to be comfortable, but also left one open to being played with.

He ran his hands over her back, pushing her hair to the side so it was out of the way. "You have such fair skin." His fingers traced her spine then caressed her pert ass. "I'm going to use a feather tickler on you then we'll play with the vibrator and egg, and then finally, the rabbit flogger."

"Yes, Sir." Her voice was strong and steady.

Cameron stepped back from her tantalizing body. He stripped off his shirt and set it on the chair before returning to her. He picked up the purple tickler and drew it across her lower back.

A giggle reached his ears, and he couldn't help but smile. He continued up and down her back and over the back of her arms. She started to rise up.

"Stay still." He placed his palm in the middle of her back, pressing her down. "I promised not to restrain you, but you need to hold your position."

"Sorry, Sir." Her body relaxed under his hand.

He stepped back. *Time to take things to the next level.* He picked up the vibrator. "Let's see if you need more of a warm up." He dipped his finger between her legs, drawing the digit through her parted pussy lips. She was wet, but not quite ready yet. He set the vibrator down and smacked her ass.

Kristen squealed.

"You need a little more warming up," he said as he gave her three more swats before soothing his hands over her pink ass. The rest of her skin was flushing. He dipped his finger between her legs. She was drenched. Keeping one hand, caressing her outer pussy lips, he reached over and picked up the vibrator.

He pressed the tip to her wet opening and pushed it in. A groan left Kristen's lips.

Kristen's breath caught in her throat as he coaxed the vibrator into her pussy. Every nerve in her body was already on alert, waiting for more. When he had used the tickler on her body it had been nice, but when Cameron spanked her ass...the delicious sensations vibrated through her body, making her hot.

Cameron didn't hit her hard. She clenched her ass slightly when he smacked her, but the sound of his palm hitting her ass had her taking a deep breath in pleasure. Now, he shifted the vibrator farther into her pussy. She clenched her inner muscles. It had been so long since she'd pleasured herself. The vibrator stopped.

"Don't stop, Sir." Thank goodness, she remembered at the last second to address him right. "Please, Sir."

The vibrator slipped into her pussy deeper but stopped again. Cameron rested his palm on her ass then the vibration came to life. Oh God, the sensations. Her pussy clenched around the toy, and her breath hiccupped in her throat.

"Ah." She started to rise up, but he slipped his palm up her spine, holding her in place. Kristen settled back down, trying to let the vibrations flow through her body. Her core muscles clenched again as if trying to draw the vibrator into her more.

"So pretty," Cameron's voice was soft.

She couldn't see him, but she heard his soft footfalls, and she imagined him pacing around her as she lay on the bench. A shiver of anticipation swept over her.

"Now, my sweet, I'm going to use a harness to hold the vibrator and another toy against your pussy, so don't panic. I will have to secure it around your waist."

"Yes, Sir." Another toy? The vibrator was on low, but its gentle vibrations were starting to create a delicious need inside her. Kristen waited as fabric encircled her waist. She fought against squirming when his fingers caressed her clit, but then something round and cool replaced his hand on her swollen bud.

His thumb pressed against the vibrator, making sure it was fully inserted in her pussy. Kristen sucked in a breath as Cameron removed his fingers, but she stiffened when the harness was pulled tight. The smooth fabric ran up the crease of her ass and was attached to the band at her waist.

"Ready?" he asked.

"For what, Sir?"

His chuckle reached her ears as he pressed his hand against her back and…

"Fuck." He'd turned on the egg, and it was a good thing his hand was on her back to hold her down. She'd almost come right off the spanking bench at the sensation coursing through her clit. Her nipples hardened to tight buds.

"Are you ready for the next phase?" he asked.

Kristen swallowed as her mouth went dry. "Next phase, Sir?" She could barely concentrate with the vibrator and egg making her pussy tighten with each vibration.

"Maybe not," he whispered in her ear. "You seem awfully tense."

She heard a rustling sound then several strands of something soft trailed over the sides of her breasts and over her sides. Her fingers curved over the end of the bench as she opened her mouth, trying to get more air into her lungs.

Cameron continued to trail whatever he held in his hand over her body. From her ass, down one leg, over the soles of her feet, up her other leg, then over her ass again.

Shivers of delight racked her body, but that didn't seem to stop Cameron. He continued to torment her. Her body was a bundle of rapture as he played with her.

"Now, you're ready," he whispered.

Before she could ask what he meant, the vibrator and the egg were turned up, and he gave a light swat on her ass, but it wasn't with his hand. No, this was different. It was a flogger. The second swat sent shockwaves of desire through her body.

The toys vibrated against each other. Her fingers squeezed the bench harder. Her nipples hurt, and flutters started in her stomach. This was so different than she could have ever imagined. There wasn't any pain, maybe a little sting, but pure pleasure coursed through her body.

Oh crap, he turned the toys up again, and her pussy muscles clenched hard against the vibrator. She wasn't going to last much longer. No. She shook her head. She didn't want to come yet. She wanted to play and play some more.

"So beautiful." Cameron's soft words were spoken against her ear. "But you're fighting your climax. Let it go."

"Can't." It was as if she had a spring inside her, coiling tighter and tighter.

"Yes, you can." The flogger hit her ass.

Her toes curled. Another hit...and her mind went blank as her orgasm roared through her, making her entire body shake.

The next thing she knew, Cameron was sitting on the sofa with her on his lap, wrapped in a blanket. He was whispering softly to her. Her head was on his shoulder. She started to move, and his arms tightened around her.

"Just rest for a bit," he said, his voice full of concern.

"I'm okay. That was just a little intense." A shiver racked her body. *Intense* barely covered it. When she'd let go and let her climax overtake her, it had been pure bliss. In a way, she thought she'd be more embarrassed with Cameron, but instead, she felt safe and secure in his arms.

"It was intense." His lips brushed her temple, his blue eyes anxious.

"Cameron." She fought to get her arm loose from the blanket he had her wrapped up in, when she did, she touched his cheek. "I've never experienced something so primal, so freeing, and so erotic."

His blue eyes lightened. He captured her hand and brought it to his lips, kissing her palm. "You are a miracle to me."

Her lips turned up then she glanced at the clock on the wall. Damn. "I really need to get home, change, and do some baking." It was almost one in the afternoon.

"Rest for a few more minutes. Then you can dress, and I'll take you home."

She didn't argue with him, she enjoyed being held in his arms like this. "What are you going to do after you take me home?"

"I'm staying with you today."

Her startled gaze clashed with his. "With me?"

"Yes. I want you to show me your baking operation."

"Why?" She tilted her head, and her lips caressed his neck.

"Because I want to know what you do."

Pleasure filled her. He was interested in her work. "All right, but don't blame me if you get bored."

"Never."

****

Cameron groaned when his alarm went off at four thirty on Monday morning. Time for him to get used to early hours again. He'd gotten used to sleeping until seven, but not now.

Bounding out of bed, he strode into the bathroom and turned on the shower. His Sunday with Kristen had been enlightening. He'd enjoyed watching her create new things. She had him taste test several items. He'd told her each one was delicious, and they were. Her skills in the kitchen were impressive.

There was something so carefree about her when she was baking. He wanted to release that into other parts of her life. This week, he was going to treat her like any other woman he was dating. While he enjoyed kink, he didn't need it every day.

After his shower, he dressed in jeans and one of the university T-shirts. He packed up his laptop, cell, notes, and drove to Kristen's cafe.

He parked in back and knocked on the door. A few seconds later, the door opened without any locks being turned.

"Good morning." Kristen grinned at him.

"Why isn't this door locked?"

She shook her head. "Deliveries." She sauntered

away from him.

"And they just walk in." He followed her.

"They knock, but if I don't answer they will open the door and bring in the products."

He frowned. "You're here alone."

"Not today." She opened the oven and pulled blueberry scones out. His stomach growled. "Quit standing there, frowning."

"It's not safe, Kristen."

"I only unlock it when I know deliveries are coming, otherwise, it stays locked." She reached beneath the counter and held up a round cylinder. "And I have pepper spray and a panic button."

Leave it to her. He held up his hands. "You've thought this through."

"Yes, and there's a bat in the corner."

He shook his head. "I apologize."

"No reason to. I do love a protective male." She crossed over to him and brushed a soft kiss against his lips. "They make me hot." With that, she danced away.

Cameron laughed. He loved her humor. But he'd pay her back.

Chapter Ten

The bell of the café rang before the lunch crowd on Thursday, and Kristen glanced up to see Cameron striding through the door. She was surprised to see him. Sunday had been fun. He'd stayed with her as she baked, asking her questions about her baking, but also about how she ran her business. He didn't try to tell her she was doing things wrong and was genuinely interested in her work. He even rubbed her shoulders and back after she was done.

No one but her grandmother had given her the support that Cameron was. It made her feel special, and she was beginning to be more relaxed around him. She let out a giggle. She enjoyed being with him, so much so. If this relationship didn't work, what she was going to do without him?

Each morning this week, Cameron had arrived at the café by five thirty, and they'd have coffee and breakfast together.

On Monday and Tuesday, Cameron had worked on his lesson plans while Kristen had baked, or he had helped in the café. On Wednesday, his classes had started, so from nine until two, he was at the university.

Today, Cameron already looked worn out so early in his day.

"Rough day?" she asked, fixing him a cup of coffee.

"All freshman today. It's always a challenge." He set his bag on what has become known as Cameron's table before he crossed over to her.

"It's only eleven thirty." She held out his coffee.

"Two full classes of freshman." He took it from her and set it on the counter. After a quick glance around, he covered her lips with his.

Kristen melted against him. Her arms slid up his, surrounding his neck as her mouth parted. His tongue darted between her lips, dueling with her tongue before roaming around her mouth.

She needed this. Their kisses were the only thing that had gotten her through this week. They'd talked over dinner, but nothing more than that. Oh he had kissed her, but no kinky play or foreplay. Nothing but kisses. She was frustrated in more ways than one. Her fingers tangled in his short hair, and when he lifted his head, she tried to pull him back. "More," she whispered.

"Later."

She pouted but removed her arms from around his neck. Cameron picked up his coffee then grinned at her. "Appearances, remember?"

Kristen puffed out a breath. Damn the man. He was taking her at her word. Why did she have to freak out over them being seen together? Habit? Well, this was one habit she was going to break, because she wanted more than just his kisses.

Tim came flying in the café door, his sandy hair disheveled and his expression anxious. "Sorry I'm late." He was out of breath.

"It's okay, Tim." She waved her hands. "We're not busy yet." The crowds would arrive shortly. It would just be her and Tim today. She'd given Skye the day off since she was working Saturday.

"Cool. I'll go change." He rounded the counter. "Hey, Cameron," Tim said before disappearing into the back.

"I guess I better get back to work," she said.

"I'll be at my table." He brushed another kiss across her lips before striding across the room and sitting down. Cameron wanted nothing more than to keep Kristen in his arms, but she had work to do, and so did he.

Cameron sipped his coffee and looked at his lesson plans. The freshman were going to take a lot of work. It seemed like kids had come to the university with less knowledge about the human body than ever before. Already, he had given two students extra homework assignments for snickering in class, and there were another four that couldn't talk without blushing.

"Hey, Cameron."

He glanced up. "Jack." Jack owned the local BDSM club and had smoothed things over for Cameron to help him regain his skills while in Scotland. Cameron stood and they shook hands. "Sit down. What are you doing here?"

Jack grinned. "I stop by now and then for coffee and a treat. You look like you've taken up residence." He waved at the laptop and papers.

"Yeah, I'm dating Kristen."

"Scotland did you good, then." Jack took a seat across from Cameron, his dark hair curling around the collar of his polo shirt.

"Yes. Thanks for setting everything up."

"No problem. You haven't been by the club."

"Not yet." Cameron's gaze found Kristen behind the counter, smiling as she talked to a customer. "I will be there soon."

"Ah, training a new one?"

"Not really." Cameron frowned. "Kristen is more than just a sub."

"No offense." Jack held his hands up. "We miss you. I'd love it if you took back over the intro classes."

Damn, he'd been neglecting the club. Was it because of Kristen? He didn't think so. He'd been pretty busy since he'd gotten home, getting ready before his classes had started at the university. He still hadn't made any progress in his decision about returning to Scotland or not. It wasn't as if he needed the money the university there was offering, but the openness to sexual matters tugged at him.

"When does the next class start?"

Jack's dark eyes lit up. "Sunday at one."

"Why the hopeful look?" Cameron asked.

"I'm shorthanded, and no one handles the intro classes as good as you do. I could really use you back to do them."

Guilt tugged at him and he made a quick decision. "I'll be there." Maybe introducing Kristen to the club before Sunday was a good idea.

"Thanks, Cameron." Jack stood up. "I've got to get back to the club. Come at eleven on Sunday, and I'll show you all the upgrades we did while you were gone."

Cameron watched Jack leave, and his gaze returned to Kristen. She was staring at him. Maybe they should go to the club tomorrow night? He could introduce her around and show her how a well-run club worked. He winked at her, and she giggled before greeting the next customer.

****

Kristen locked the café door promptly at six. It had been a long afternoon, but Cameron had stayed keeping busy with grading class work. She leaned against the door and looked at Cameron. "Who was the guy talking to you earlier?"

"Jack Christenson."

"He owns the gas station, right?" She turned off the lights as they walked into the kitchen.

"Among other things, yes." He let out a chuckle.

"Other things?"

"Jack runs Decadence."

Her cheeks flushed. "The BDSM club? But he looks so normal."

Cameron burst out laughing. "Are you saying I don't?"

"No, that's not what I meant." She shook her head.

"Come on, finish locking up, and we'll talk over dinner."

He helped her clean up and get things ready for the morning. Then he drove them to a local restaurant. Thirty minutes later, they were seated at a Mexican restaurant. "Now tell me about what you meant about Jack."

Kristen looked down at her hands then back up at him. "I just thought he'd be all black leather and boots."

Cameron smiled. "Jack does wear leather pants at the club. How he stands them, I'll never know. They're hotter than Hell." He reached across the table and took her hand in his. He'd chosen this restaurant, because they kept their tables spread apart with lots of space between them. Plus, they never rushed customers to eat or leave.

"Will you tell me more about the club?" Kristen asked.

"What do you want to know?" He was happy she was curious.

"Everything."

"Tall order." He was glad he had asked for a table in the corner on the outside terrace. The night was cool, but not cold. The trees blocked any wind, creating an intimate setting. There was less chance of them being overheard. "Decadence is what I'd call a medium-sized club. It is membership based."

"Does one just apply?"

"Sometimes. But most of the time a person is sponsored by another member."

"And just how many members are there?"

"Hundreds." When her jaw dropped open, he laughed. "Not everyone is local. There are members from other cities plus several long-distance members."

"Why?"

"Why what?"

"Long-distance members. What do they get out of it?"

"A place to belong." He entwined his fingers with hers. "We try hard to build a community, a place where people understand that no matter what their kink is, they can feel open and free to share it within reason."

"Within reason? So are some things the club doesn't allow?"

"Yes. No blood play, no water sports, no sex."

Kristen swallowed. "No sex?"

"Not on the club floor. We have some private

rooms, but there are rules we have to obey."

"Got it." She tilted her head and stared at him. "You haven't been to the club since you got home, have you?"

"No." He squeezed her fingers. "Jack asked me to start teaching the intro class again."

"Is that what you did there?"

"Among other things, yes. I teach the newer members what to expect at the club, the rules, and what will happen if they don't follow the rules." He loved teaching the classes to help those who wanted kink in their lives.

Cameron gazed at Kristen's face. Her eyes were bright with curiosity, and she kept tilting her head from side to side. "Would you like to go to the club tomorrow night?"

Her hand jerked in his. "Would Jack allow it?"

"You'd be my guest, and it would be easy enough to make you a member."

"Umm…" She bit her lower lip.

"If it's too soon for you to go to the club, just say so."

"No." She gave him a smile. "I'd like to see the club and sit in on your class."

"Good. It means taking Friday and Saturday night off from baking."

Kristen's shoulder drooped. "I can do that, but…"

"What's going on?"

"I have six big orders coming on Friday for Saturday. There's no way I'm going to get them all done if we go to the club tomorrow night, so that means I work tonight."

"Can't Skye or someone else help you tomorrow?"

She shook her head. "I'm sorry. I just don't trust the baking to anyone else."

Cameron took a deep breath. How would he feel about having someone else prep a class he was expected to teach? "I get it." He wouldn't be comfortable, nor would he be confident in what he was teaching if someone else prepped for him.

"Thanks." She gave him a small smile.

"Kristen." He waited until her gaze met his. "Communication. You don't have to be afraid to tell me you need to work. I just don't want you using it as an excuse."

"It's not."

"Good." He released her hand when their food was delivered. After the waiter walked away, he grinned at her. "Eat. I'll take you back to the café, and you can explain these big orders coming in at the café."

Chapter Eleven

A primal beat thrummed in the background of the club, making Kristen's body pulse in time to the music. She glanced around the waiting room where she and Cameron stood. It held sofas, chairs, and a fridge. On one wall was a counter with two coffee pots and hot water on warming plates. A stack of paper cups were next to the drinks along with a pile of napkins and some small paper plates. A couple of trays of fruit and veggies were spread out on the counter.

"Hey, Cameron, I didn't expect to see you tonight." Jack's voice was happy. He wore a pair of black leather pants, and his chest was bare.

"Hey, Jack." The two men embraced. Kristen glanced down. Jack's feet were bare, and she wondered why. Plus, he wore black and yellow arm bands on his bicep and a black band on his wrist.

When they pulled apart, Jack's brown eyes focused in on her. She shifted from one foot to the other. "Hello, Kristen."

"Hello," she said, unsure what to call him. Jack? Sir?

"Out here, you can call me Jack, but inside the club, it's Sir." He took her hand and brought it to his lips, placing a kiss on her knuckles.

"Quit making eyes at her." Cameron punched Jack in the arm.

Jack released her hand with a laugh and a wink. "We've got a pretty light group tonight."

"Good. We're going to sit out here for a while and give Kristen a chance to acclimate to the club."

"I'm sure you won't lack for company. I'm glad you're back." Jack nodded in her direction then disappeared into the other room.

"Let's go sit down." Cameron gestured to one of the unoccupied sofas. There were only two other people in the room, and they were at the other end of the area on a sofa, kissing.

Kristen lowered herself onto the cream-colored sofa. Cameron sat down next to her, his thigh resting solidly against hers. "So this is like a waiting area?" she asked.

"Sort of." He picked up her hand and entwined their fingers. "Many come out here to have a little alone time or to settle down after a scene. In some cases, to talk."

"Talk about what?"

"There are unattached subs and Doms, and they will come out here to negotiate their scene before they actually play."

"That makes sense."

"Since it's Friday night, it means the club is open to members, their guests, and new members."

"So?"

"It's easier to talk out here rather than in the club itself. Plus it allows people who aren't sure about entering the club time to feel comfortable without being pressured."

"Oh." She hadn't seen that before. "What do the bands on Jack's arm mean?"

"Each band has a special meaning." He lifted his arm, showing her the black one around his bicep. "Black means Master in the club."

"Master?"

"You read the book I gave you?"

"I did." She pressed her lips together as she tried to remember everything she'd read. "But you said Master, not Dom."

"Correct." He grinned. "When Jack started the club, he wanted to focus more on education about BDSM and the community." Cameron moved closer to her. "But he also wanted a place where people could play. Where they would be safe to play."

"Is that why I had to fill out the application? Show my driver's license and answer the questions on the application, such as if I'd ever been arrested?" She was starting to understand more about safe, sane, and consensual.

"Yes. While we do allow guests, we have to limit liability for the safety of our guests."

"Okay, so a Dom is also a Master?" She might get the hang of this.

He shook his head, and she scrunched up her nose. "A Master in this context is a Master in the club only. The position holder is usually a Dom as well, but a Master is here to keep the peace. If he has a yellow band on his bicep, like Jack does, he is also a dungeon monitor, who will watch the scenes, make sure nothing gets out of hand, and will take care of any problems before they become extreme."

"So the Dungeon Masters are like monitors?" This was so different from what she'd experienced before and made her feel safer.

"Sort of, although there are a few monitors as well. They will have yellow bands on their biceps. On nights when the club is really full, we need the help."

"How many Masters are there?"

"Let's see…Jack, me, my brothers and—"

"Your bothers are into this as well?" She winced as her voice rose. Glancing around, she was glad to see there wasn't anyone close to them. Holy crap. Was his whole family into it? What about Skye?

"Yes, but we don't discuss it over the dinner table." He grinned at her, his blue eyes sparkling with mischief. "Remember our conversation about how being part of the lifestyle is being discreet." He touched her cheek. "And before you ask, yes, our parents are well aware of our activities. We have their approval."

"Your family is so open and supportive." She hated the wishful tone in her voice. Her parents had only cared about her when it had benefited them.

"They are. So, this means that a Master's word in the club is law."

"Do you…" She didn't know how to ask the question, so instead, she held up her wrist. "I have a white band."

"It signifies you are a guest of an attending club member." He glanced up as a couple walked into the room, and he gave a nod in greeting before turning his attention back to her. "Wrist bands are like this—black is a Dom or Domme. Green with red means the sub likes pain. Green with blue means the sub likes a little pain. Just green is a sub."

"I'm never going to remember all this." Her brain was already overflowing.

"You don't need to tonight. I want you to

understand what happens in the club before we go in."

"You don't expect me to..." Kristen swallowed, her gaze landing on a woman who walked into the lounge area from the club, wearing only a thong.

Cameron glanced up then turned his attention back to her. "You can stay as dressed or get as undressed as you want. You'll see everything in the club."

Kristen nodded, her brain swirling with questions and fears. "No sex in the club, right?"

"Correct. Only in the private rooms. Those rooms have to be negotiated ahead of time. No cell phones, no cameras, and no recording devices."

"How do you enforce all that?"

"Remember when you filled out the form, I had asked you to give me your purse?"

"Yes." She thought it was odd at the time, but she hadn't questioned him.

"Behind the desk there is a set of small lockers. You have to surrender all personal items. They're put in there."

"How do they know what belongs to who?"

"Each locker has a slot, and your name is slipped into the slot."

"That makes sense, but..." There was a loud, sharp snap, and Kristen jumped. A moan followed. It didn't sound like a moan of pain, but she wasn't sure.

Cameron's blood heated at the sound of a flogger hitting skin. "Someone is being flogged," Cameron explained. He hoped bringing Kristen here wouldn't set her training back. The club could be intense at times. He'd watch her carefully to make sure she wasn't overwhelmed.

"And that moan?"

"It sounded like Amber." He grinned as Kristen frowned. "As a Master, I know the subs and their sounds." It amazed him that after being gone for six months, he could still identify them. "Are you okay?"

"Fine. This is very different." Her eyes were wide, but her body was relaxed.

"From what?" He wanted to know what she was thinking.

"The club I was taken to was dark, the music loud, and there was nothing wrong with having sex out in the open."

He remembered her telling him about the club. He wanted her to know Decadence was different and she was safe here. "Our lighting is subdued, but not dark. Music is used to enhance the mood, and I've already stated no sex. But you may see other things."

"Like what?" She tilted her head.

"Varying amounts of nudity, toys being used, and bondage." He stood and pulled her to her feet. "Let's go walk around. I want you to experience things." If she couldn't handle the club, then he would have to adjust his plans about them playing there in the future.

"One more question." She tugged on his hand.

"Yes." He gazed at her.

Her face was flushed, her breathing a little rapid, and her eyes held questions. "What was the yellow band around Jack's arm?"

"You are very observant. All monitors wear them." He ran a finger down her hot cheek. "Safe, sane, consensual. You are safe."

She nodded and let out a breath. "I'm ready."

Cameron leaned down and brushed a light kiss over her lips. "If you get overwhelmed or frightened, tell me, and we'll come out here to sit."

"I will." She gazed up at him. "I trust you."

He stared at her as his heart beat in his ears. "I won't violate that trust." He took her hand and led her into the club.

Chapter Twelve

Kristen blinked several times as Cameron guided her into the main club. This wasn't like anything she'd imagined. People milled around. Some of the women were dressed, and some only wore a thong. The men all wore pants; some were shirtless while others had on tank tops or no shirts. The only drinks she saw were bottles of water. And people were talking to each other, not just standing around watching.

It was very open, had lots of stations, and… She was a little bit overwhelmed. "Wow," she whispered. "It's so open and big."

"Compared to?"

"The one I was taken to was so industrial. Not a lot of open space."

"Not here." He tucked her against him. "We like space for demos and so people can watch while others play."

"What kinds of demos?" She tilted her head back and looked at him. She expected the room to smell of sweat and sex, but instead, it had a fresh, clean scent. But the night was young.

"Flogging, whipping." He maneuvered her until her back was against his chest, his arms wrapped around her waist.

A couple in front of them moved away from the scene, and she barely prevented a gasp from leaving her lips. In front of her was a large massage table where a nude woman lay. Two muscular men in black pants stood over her.

"This is probably the most vanilla station," Cameron whispered in her ear. "It's our massage area. Both Doms and subs use it."

One of the men picked up a bottle and poured some of the contents into his palm before handing it off to the other. Hands descended onto the woman's back, and she let out a moan of pleasure as they began to knead her shoulders.

"The two men are Paul and Will. Their day job is massage therapy."

"Don't they own Hot Rock Massage?" She was sure they'd been to her café a couple of times.

"Yes." She shifted, and Cameron tightened his hold on her waist. "Is something bothering you?"

"No, it's…" What? She shook her head. "Preconceived notions rearing their little heads." The woman's eyes were closed, and every so often, she'd moan in bliss. There was nothing wrong with this.

"Paul and Will enjoy their jobs, which is why they volunteer here. The massage can be as vanilla or as sexual as the person wants."

"You mentioned Doms getting massages as well."

"If a Dom wants one, then yes. They have April." He gestured to a woman who was sitting behind the group. "She is one of their female assistants. She does most of the men."

"That makes sense."

"Would you like to try?" Cameron raised his hand.

"Ummm."

"You don't have to remove your clothing at all.

They'll understand."

The woman slid off the table and stood with Will's help. Another man strode up to the pair, smiled at Will, and took the woman in his arms. He kissed her deeply before they walked off.

"Cameron," Paul said.

Several heads turned in their direction, and Kristen shrank against Cameron. She really didn't want all this attention.

"It's okay." He guided her to the front as several people welcomed him back to the club. "Paul, this is Kristen. I'd like her to have a relaxing massage."

Kristen smiled and held her hand out to the beefy blond man.

"I love your mini quiches," Paul said, taking her hand.

"Thank you." She forced air into her lungs. What was she doing? She should just tell Cameron she couldn't do this, but a massage would be heaven.

Paul gestured to the table. "When you're ready, just hop up on the table. Will has already cleaned it."

"Yeah, well…" She glanced up at Cameron.

"Kristen is new and would like to stay dressed."

Paul frowned. "The jeans are fine, but it would be easier without the blouse she's wearing."

Will stepped forward. "We can hold a towel up, and you can slip your top off. We'll make sure the towel is wrapped around you. Then once you lay down, we'll unfold it so we can get to your lovely skin."

"We'll even face the other way as you take your blouse off if that helps," Paul said.

She took a shaky breath in relief. "That would be fine."

Paul grabbed a towel and handed one side to Will. They faced the audience as Cameron guided her behind them.

"I don't need help," she said.

"I'm going to be right here with you, protecting what is mine."

Cameron's possessive tone sent a shiver of desire up her spine. She quickly undid the buttons of her shirt and slipped it off. Cameron took the fabric from her fingers and draped it over his shoulder then nudged her forward until her bra touched the towel.

His heat singed her back as he wrapped the towel around her torso. "All set." He flashed her a grin and led her over to the table. "Lay down and be comfortable. I'll be right here, watching."

"Yes, Sir." Kristen closed her eyes, only to flinch when hands skimmed her skin as the towel was opened.

"Easy," Paul whispered, his voice soft. "Don't be frightened. It's just us."

"Relax, Kristen. We'll take good care of you," Will added.

Easy for them to say. They didn't have people watching, waiting…waiting for what? There was nothing wrong with the situation. She'd had massages before, and there had been other people in the room. But this was different.

She blew out a breath and concentrated on relaxing her muscles.

"That's it," Paul said.

Two sets of hands went to work on her. One set kneaded her shoulders and another rubbed at the small of her back. With each press of their fingers into her muscles, her body relaxed more and more.

Oh Lord, this felt so good. She bent over to get goodies in and out of the ovens all day, plus leaning over the counter to decorate a cake. She should probably get a massage more often.

Thumbs pressed into her spine as hands slipped down her legs, massaging through her jeans. The hands hesitated at her feet.

"I'm going to remove your shoes," Will said.

"Sure," she whispered, floating on a blissful cloud of lax muscles.

Her shoes were whisked off. Her right foot was flexed several times before Will's fingers began to work their magic. A moan of pleasure slipped past her lips.

"That's it, Kristen," Paul whispered. "Just feel, let your body go. Let us do all the work and make you feel good."

"We're done."

Will's voice startled Kristen. She had no idea of how much time had passed. She'd been lost in the pleasure of the massage.

"I don't think I can move," she said. Every part of her objected at the thought of moving.

"Take your time," Will said.

"Kristen," Cameron whispered, his breath brushing her cheek.

She turned her head and opened her eyes. "Hi. That was wonderful."

"Good." He folded the towel over her back and helped her sit up. "Okay?" he asked as he drew her to her feet.

"Yes." She was grateful he held on to her as her legs were a bit wobbly. He led her off to the side and held the towel up as she put her blouse back on. When she was dressed, she walked back over to Paul and Will. "Thank you both."

"Our pleasure." They both smiled at her.

Cameron slipped his arm around her waist and guided her back to the lounge. Once there, she slid down onto one of the love seats. She couldn't remember the last time she had felt this relaxed.

The cushion dipped next to her as Cameron sat down. She tilted her head to look at him. He was grinning. He twisted the cap off of the bottle of water he held and handed it to her.

"Drink."

She took a couple of deep sips. "I think I'm in heaven."

He chuckled. "I'll have to make sure I add massage to my repertoire."

"You do that, and I'll never get out of your hair."

"Consider it a deal."

"What's next?" How would it feel to have Cameron's hands massaging her back? Shivers of anticipation flowed through her. Somehow, she had a feeling it would be considerably more erotic than the massage she just had. She polished off the water.

"When you're ready, we'll got back in and walk around. I want you to feel comfortable at the club."

"I'm ready." She stood.

Cameron led her back into the room and over to a flogging station. A blonde-haired woman was tied to the Saint Andrews cross, and Jack stood next to her. After a minute, Kristen realized the woman was nude. Funny, after the first couple of people, she never really noticed who was dressed and who wasn't. Everyone was so open and friendly that it didn't matter.

"All right, everyone. This is Piper. She volunteered to be my sub for this demonstration," Jack said.

Kristen shifted, and Cameron pulled her in front of him, giving her an unobstructed view.

"For those of you who have never flogged anyone before, I will be giving a flogging class every Saturday from one to two for the next six weeks." Jack paced as he talked. "You just can't pick up a flogger and starting hitting someone. That's the quickest way to hurt your sub and yourself."

Cameron slipped his arms around her waist and pulled her against him. The warmth of his body seeped into hers, and she relaxed into his embrace, enjoying the feel of his arms around her.

"If your sub has never been flogged before, I suggest starting with something simple." He held up a small flogger. "A rabbit hair flogger or something similar." Jack turned and began striking the flogger against Piper's ass. "Remember it's important not to constantly flog the same place and to always avoid the lower back where the kidneys are, the spine, the head, and knees."

"Notice Piper's skin," Cameron whispered in her ear. "Her ass has a nice, light-pink hue to it."

Kristen nodded as Jack welded the flogger. There was something hypnotic in the way the flogger swung back and forth, and the gentle swishing sound soothing.

"Blood is rushing to the area," Cameron said quietly, "making it more sensitive."

Heat filled her veins, and her skin danced with anticipation. How would it feel to have Cameron flog her? She shifted, and his erection pressed up against her ass. He was aroused, and she was getting there.

"No matter how experienced the sub is with flogging, always warm them up." Jack rubbed Piper's ass. "How are you doing, Piper?"

"Green, Sir."

"You'll learn in class to always check in with your sub and how to watch your sub. If they go into subspace, they're not going to call out their safeword if it gets to be too much. Plus, you'll need to watch for Domspace as well."

"Excuse me, Master Jack. What is Domspace?" someone asked.

"Domspace is just like subspace, except the Dom loses all awareness of time and space. I'm not saying it will happen but to be aware. I've seen more floggings go bad because the Dom wasn't aware." He glanced around the crowd. "Now, let's move on."

By the time Jack was finished with his demonstration, Kristen was aroused beyond belief. Her core throbbed, her clit ached, and her nipples were hard, little points under the corset she wore.

If they hadn't been in the club, she would have begged Cameron to take her.

Cameron's erection still pressed against the crease of her ass. On occasion, his dick had jerked in his pants.

She faced Cameron, her body on fire.

He gazed at her, his dark eyes blazing. "I..."

The crowd was breaking up, the others moving to other stations, some finding sofas to fondle each other.

"Tell me what you want." His voice was husky with desire and need.

"Relief." It was the first word that came into her mind.

His eyebrows rose.

"Relief, Sir."

"Better." He glanced over her shoulder. "Jack, I need a room, please."

"Room four," Jack said.

Cameron nodded, and taking her by the hand, he strode through the club to the back where there were six doors. He opened the fourth one and pulled Kristen inside. The door slid shut, and he released her.

"Cameron?" She faced him as he leaned against the door.

"Private room."

"Oh." She turned. The room wasn't really decorated. There was a throw rug in the middle, a four-poster bed on one wall, a dresser on another, and a single chair along the side. "Not much for decoration, are they?"

"No."

She jumped when his breath brushed her cheek.

"Strip for me and get on the bed," he ordered.

"Yes, Sir." Her heart thumped in her chest as she slipped away from him and began undressing. A shiver slid over her skin from the cool air of the room and her own excitement. After folding her clothes and setting them on the dresser, she went over to the bed. Were the sheets clean?

"Why the hesitation?"

"Sorry, Sir. Are the sheets clean?"

A grin slid over his lips. "Yes, they're changed and the room is cleaned after each use."

Kristen inclined her head. "Thank you, Sir." With a wiggle of her ass, she climbed onto the mattress. Cameron knelt on the bed before she had time to be nervous.

"Tell me what you thought about Jack's demonstration." He leaned over and began running kisses along her collar bone, the top of her breasts, and between them.

"Uh..." He expected her to think while he was caressing her skin? "It was interesting."

"In what way?"

A groan escaped her lips. "I've never seen a flogging so sensual." It was the only word she could come up with, because it fit. Jack wielded the whips with care and precision but also with passion and flare.

"Continue," Cameron said as he kissed his way down her right leg before switching to her left.

"Piper had squirmed and moaned, but she never looked like she was in pain."

During the demonstration, Piper's face had been filled with pure bliss. Oh, she had wiggled and squirmed on the cross, but no tears and no fear had radiated from her—just pleasure and desire.

"And that's how it should be." Cameron's breath caressed her ankle. "Pleasure with a little bit of pain."

"Earlier, we heard someone cry out."

"Amber. Do you remember the sound?" Cameron fingers danced over her skin around her stomach and thighs, making it hard to concentrate.

"She had moaned."

"Yes, again from pleasure, not pain." He rose over her.

Kristen thought on his words. Yes, so far everything she had seen was about pleasure and not pain, not humiliation. "It's all so different."

"From?" he asked before lowering his mouth to her

breasts.

"What I've seen before." Her hands fluttered to his back, and her palms met skin. When had he taken off his shirt? Hot, wet heat flowed into her from his lips, caressing her breasts.

Cameron lifted his head. "Good." His left hand toyed with her right nipple. Desire shot from her nipple to her clit. "I know the flogging aroused you."

"Yes." Her back arched when he pinched her nipple. "It was playful and sensual."

"I was aroused, too, but only because I held you in my arms." His body rose over hers, and the silkiness of his pants teased her skin.

"You still have your pants on." She frowned.

"Yes, this is for you." He captured her lips in a kiss before kissing his way down her body again. He pushed her legs apart, lifting them to his shoulders.

"Cameron?" Oh hell. Her stomach tightened with anticipation. She wasn't expecting this.

"Shhh." His eyes flashed with wickedness as he lowered his head to her core.

When he flicked his tongue against her pussy, she cried out. The sensation had her tightening her pussy muscles. Her eyes closed in bliss as he licked her.

Cameron shifted on the mattress, opening her to his explorations.

"Oh God," she said as his tongue found her clit and began to play with it. A tremor went though her body. She only had one boyfriend try to go down on her, and it had been just shy of a disaster.

But Cameron? Her neck arched as he licked around her pussy, tasting and using his tongue to make her nerves dance. Her pussy fluttered with her growing orgasm.

What? She couldn't be on the edge of a climax already, could she? The more Cameron licked and sucked, the stronger the flutters grew. That had never happened to her before.

"Cameron. Sir." Her fingers clutched the sheets. But he didn't pause. He kept at his work until she was squirming uncontrollably on the mattress. When she though she couldn't take anymore, he pushed two fingers into her pulsing core.

She cried out as an orgasm ripped through her, her clit pulsing in time with the ripples flowing through her pussy. As the tremors passed, Cameron lowered her back onto the mattress and kissed his way back up her body. He gathered her into his arms and rolling onto his back.

Her rapid breathing ruffled his chest hair as she lay against him.

"Rest for a bit. Then, we'll go see what is happening in the club."

"But—" She started to raise her head, but his hand pressed against the back of the skull.

"Rest, and remember, this is for you."

Chapter Thirteen

Kristen paced around her apartment Sunday morning. On Saturday, Cameron had picked her up, and they had spent the day at his house. That time in his playroom, she hadn't frozen up. She let out a laugh.

After the bliss he had given her Friday night at the Club, how could she freeze up? The man was as good of a masseur as Paul and Will were. She had been putty in his hands after that. But Cameron hadn't taken advantage. Oh, he had tied her up and teased her with a feather and a soft rabbit flogger, but that was it.

Then they had spent the rest of Saturday afternoon kissing, caressing, and cuddling on his sofa. When she had arrived home last night, she had still been in full-bliss mode. This morning, she had woken with renewed energy.

Today, she was nervous and excited. They were going to the club in broad daylight today. What would happen if someone saw her walking into Decadence? Would they stop coming to her café? Would they start rumors? She couldn't start her business all over again in a new town. And she didn't have it in her to walk away from what she'd built here. But she didn't want to give up what she had found with Cameron, either.

Her heart pounded in her chest. She hadn't stepped a toe out of line in Grant in the four years she'd lived here. Now, she was making a big leap, but she deserved to be happy. Grant was a pretty progressive town. It had to be to allow the BDSM club, but still she worried about what people would think. How would they treat her if they found out she liked kink? *Oh, stop it.* She couldn't stop what people thought or how they acted. She could only control herself.

She glanced at the clock. Cameron would be here any second, and she wasn't sure what she was going to say to him. Would he understand her apprehension about them being seen at the club in daylight? The club was in a discreet location, but it was during the day now, and being there at night hadn't worried her so much. Would he think she was being silly?

She paced from one end of her living room to the other, pondering Cameron's reaction. A herd of elephants roamed around in her stomach. She should cancel. Or talk Cameron into just staying home today. But did she really want to miss this chance to attend Cameron's class and be with him?

The doorbell made her jump. Kristen smoothed her hands down her jean-clad thighs before crossing the room. She looked out the peephole and saw Cameron. She took a deep breath and let it out before opening the door.

"Good day, Kristen." Cameron's whiskey-smooth voice caused her nerves to dance with anticipation.

"Come on in." She held the door open. The faint scent of sandalwood tickled her nose as he brushed by her.

"You're nervous," he stated.

"Very intuitive of you." She closed the door and leaned against it. "I think I might have passed nervous and gone right to scared."

"Hey." Warm palms cupped her face, lifting it until their gazes met. "Nothing will happen that you don't want to."

"I…" She closed her eyes. How could she tell him how important it was to have her lifestyle remain private?

"Kristen. Open. Your. Eyes. Now."

Her lashes rose at the tone of his voice, so strong and commanding. She reacted to it without thinking.

"I know I'm pushing you a bit, but it's time."

"I'm fine," she whispered.

"Honesty, Kristen." He tucked her against his warm chest.

"I'm scared to death." Oh Lord, her heart pounded at being this close to him. She was like a giddy teenager instead of a woman in her thirties.

"Of what? Me? The club?"

"I'm not scared of you." Her lips turned up into a smile. Her attraction to Cameron wasn't something she was afraid of.

"The club?" His fingers traced up and down her spine, sending fine shivers of desire through her veins. "You didn't seem this afraid on Friday night."

"I wasn't, but…"

His fingers touched her lips as he pulled back. "Let's go sit down for a minute." He tugged her over to her sofa. But instead of letting her sit down, he pulled her onto his lap. Her body cradled against his.

Kristen squirmed. She was still getting used to be so close to Cameron. His instant need for closeness wasn't new to her. And she enjoyed having his strong arms around her.

"Sit still." His tone was firm, and she stilled.

"Now, look at me."

She tilted her head up and smiled. There was nothing but kindness in his deep-blue eyes.

"What questions are lurking in that beautiful brain of yours?" he asked.

"What happens if someone we know sees us? What does the university think about you playing at the club? What will my customers think?" The questions flowed out in a flood of words.

Cameron laughed. "That's an awful lot of questions, sweetheart." He ran his palm up and down her spine in a comforting motion. "Let me try and answer them for you. First off, if someone sees us, it doesn't matter. We're consenting adults, and it's no one's business but ours. With me on that?"

"Yes, but I worry it will affect my business."

This time he smiled, and the impact of that sexy grin went straight to her core.

"About a quarter of your customers dabble at the club, so I wouldn't worry about that. Remember the paperwork you signed Friday? We don't discuss the patrons of the club. We don't have to share what happens inside the club with anyone. I respect your need for privacy."

"But you've talked to me about it." She frowned.

"We talked about BDSM and Decadence but not about who goes there."

"Okay." She let out a breath. Maybe she was overreacting a bit.

"As for the university, I teach sexual health, including alternative lifestyles. They are well aware of it all, so there's no issue there."

Kristen opened her mouth, but he shook his head,

135

so she closed it and waited.

"Jack told me they've made some upgrades to the club, so he'll take us on a tour first. The only thing happening today is the intro class." He cupped her cheek. "Friday night was Friday night. Today isn't about playing at the club."

Some of the tension seeped out of her body at his words. It was time to trust herself again.

"You will have to fill out some additional paperwork to become a member. But today is nothing but the class."

"What kind of paperwork?" None of the clubs she'd been to had asked her for much beyond her license to prove she was over eighteen. "What about what I filled out the other night?

"The other night was just for a one-time visit. Today is for full membership paperwork. Nothing is too intrusive, and there is a strict privacy clause." His hand smoothed down her back.

"So what happens in the club stays in the club."

"Yes. As I said before, there are many members in town who belong to the club. While we may acknowledge each other outside Decadence, we generally don't discuss activities in public."

"Okay." Maybe she was making too big of deal over this, but then she reminded herself she had a right to her feelings, and Cameron wasn't dismissing them.

"The main thing to remember is everything in the club is safe, sane, and consensual."

A mantra she'd been running through her head since Friday night. She nodded. The tension slowly left her body as she sat on his lap. "I feel better now."

"Good. Are you okay with becoming a member

and attending the class today?"

"Yes." He'd answered all her questions. He didn't try to coax her into going. He had let her make her own decision.

"But first…" Cameron said. He cupped her chin, and his head dipped.

Cool, firm lips settled over hers in a too-short kiss. She tried to followed his lips as he pulled back, not wanting to lose contact.

"Later." Cameron lifted her to her feet and gave her a little swat on her ass.

"Ohh." Kristen's blood heated. He'd said they weren't going to play at the club, but his playfulness made her hopeful that maybe later tonight, they could have some fun.

"Let's go." He took her hand and pulled her out the door.

****

Within ten minutes, Cameron and Kristen arrived at Decadence and stood outside. "Appropriate name," she commented, thinking back to Friday night.

The club was on the outskirts of town with plenty of parking. Kristen thought it was interesting that Grant had a BDSM club; she'd have to ask him about it later.

"Yeah, Jack thought so." He slipped his arm around her waist and guided her inside.

Kristen was surprised to see a man and a woman sitting behind a large table with two computers on it and several stacks of paper. Friday night, she'd been so nervous she hadn't really paid that close of attention to the people at the desk.

"Hey, Cameron, nice to have you back," the woman said.

"Thanks, Piper."

Kristen's head jerked at the name. *Piper*. This was the woman Jack had demonstrated on Friday night? She looked so normal. She was dressed in jeans and a T-shirt, and her strawberry-blonde hair framed her heart-shaped face. Nothing about her screamed submissive. Kristen shook her head to dispel some preconceived notions.

Cameron's arm tightened around her waist. "This is Kristen, and she needs new member paperwork."

"Cool. Jack mentioned you might have a new member for me today." Piper pulled out a piece of paper and a pen. "Fill this out, and come back with your license. I'll get you all set up."

Cameron took the items and led Kristen over to a small table. He held out the chair, and she sat down.

"Standard stuff," he told her as he set the paper down. "Just name, address, and a few questions for you to answer. You fill this out while I get checked in."

Kristen nodded, but she watched as he sauntered back to the table where Piper sat. The tight black pants molded his ass, and a sigh of pleasure escaped her lips. Damn, she wanted to get inside those pants of his.

Cameron had a way of making her hot. Sometimes, her body vibrated with need to have her way with this hunky guy of hers. A quiet groan left her lips. As much as she'd like to stare at his ass all afternoon, she had paperwork to fill out.

The questions were different. *Have you ever been convicted as a felon?* That was a big no. *What name do you want to be called?* She left it blank to ask Cameron what they meant.

She hesitated at the next box. They were asking for

permission to run a background check. No reason not to. She'd legally changed her name when she moved to Washington.

When she finished the application, she pulled her license out and walked to the table.

Cameron was putting on a black wristband as she approached. "All finished?"

"I think so. I don't understand what they mean by *what name do I want to be called.*"

Cameron smiled, and Piper gave a giggle. "Just put down your first name if you don't have a nickname."

"Oh." Kristen's hand shook as she wrote her name. When she finished, Cameron captured her hand, removed the pen, and brought her hand to his lips.

"No need to be nervous," he whispered as Piper began typing into the computer.

"I…" Kristen took a deep breath. She had promised him honesty. "I feel a little silly not knowing what that meant."

"Some people like to be called by a nickname or pet name instead of their first name. I'm proud you asked." He slipped his arm around her waist and drew her close.

"License, please," Piper said.

Kristen gave it to her.

Piper looked it over and then handed it back. "You're all set. I'll have the new member packet ready for you when you leave."

"Thanks, Piper." Cameron settled his arm around Kristen's waist and guided her down the hallway to another door.

They entered the room, and Kristen pressed her lips together before a laugh could escape. She wasn't expecting the room to look so normal. There were chairs set up in the front, and tables pushed to the back with a coffee and tea service set up on a long bar where Jack stood alone.

Cameron said, "This is our classroom and meeting area."

"Hey, Cameron." Jack strode toward them, and the two men embraced.

Jack was dressed similar to Cameron—black pants, black shirt. What was it with these men and black?

When they pulled apart, Jack focused on her. She changed position from one foot to the other.

"Welcome back, Kristen," Jack said. "Nice to know we didn't scare you away."

"I was never scared. A bit overwhelmed but that's it, Sir."

Jack chuckled. "Don't need to be formal today, and I'm glad you weren't scared. I take it you enjoyed my demonstration Friday night?"

Heat invaded her face at his question. "Umm, yes. It was interesting."

Jack laughed then turned to Cameron, and Kristen let out a sigh of relief. Sometimes, Jack's stare made her feel like she was bug under a microscope.

Jack said, "We've got about ten people coming for class today."

"Not bad."

Jack nodded. "Yeah. Why don't I show you around? You probably didn't see everything when you were here on Friday night."

"I don't understand." Kristen glanced between Jack and Cameron. "You've been here before."

"We made some upgrades while Cameron was in

140

Scotland. Friday night, you two didn't get all the way around the room." Jack's voice had a commanding tone to it.

"Really?" Kristen lowered her gaze. Oh hell, had she spoken out of turn by asking a question? He'd said they didn't need to be formal.

Cameron cupped her chin and lifted it until she looked into his eyes. "No need to be embarrassed. If there's anything you need explained, ask."

Kristen nodded, but she couldn't stop her cheeks from turning red. She bit her lip when Cameron tried to hide his grin.

"One of the things we've done is tightened our membership policy," Jack said.

"Have you had problems?" Cameron curled his arm around Kristen's waist as they began to walk to the main section of the club.

"Minor ones, but they still needed to be addressed." Jack pushed open the heavy wooden door. "If an applicant isn't sponsored by a member, they have to attend four orientation classes. Today is the first day of that rule."

"What happened?" Cameron gestured for Kristen to walk through the doorway ahead of him.

She gasped. Her breath caught in her throat as her skin tingled with amazement. She stopped cold in her tracks.

"Not what you were expecting?" He nudged her farther into the room. "I like the new layout," he said to Jack.

"This is much bigger than I expected," Kristen gazed darted around the room, noting the high ceiling and the lighting along with the equipment. It seemed so much larger in full light than it had Friday night.

"Yeah. If we get much bigger I'll need to expand."

"Expansion is a good problem to have." Cameron glanced down at Kristen.

"As to your question about problems," Jack said. "We had a couple of bad members who started creating a fuss."

"I heard something about that a couple of months ago," Kristen said. "Two men got into a fight. There were knives involved." She took a deep breath to calm her racing heart. Seeing the club in full lighting caused excitement to race over her skin.

Jack nodded. "They were fairly new members, and they knew the rules. The two never would have made it past the second orientation."

"Makes sense," Cameron said. "You'll have to bring me up to speed on the new requirements."

"Will do, because I'm hoping to get you to permanently teach the classes. I'm stretched pretty thin. Why don't you show Kristen around?" Jack gestured with his arm toward the first station. "Since it's lit up, I'm sure she'll appreciate the tour."

Cameron curved his arm around Kristen's waist again and guided her over to the first piece of equipment with Jack following. Cameron pointed to the white lines on the floor. "The lines on the floor denote the scene space. You don't cross them when someone is in a scene."

Kristen nodded. "I noticed on Friday night that everyone stayed behind them."

"I think you know what this piece of equipment is."

"Yeah, it's a spanking bench. Pretty standard." She

did remember seeing a woman tied up on it. A part of her wondered how she'd look tied up there with Cameron welding a flogger.

"Then why the gasp earlier?" Cameron asked.

"It looks very different in the daylight, and it surprised me." That was the best explanation she had, because she really hadn't expected the club to look and feel so different in the daytime. How could she explain it? Friday night had been exciting, but today was more tantalizing.

"Could be because there are independent dimmer switches, but I prefer a little more light than others. It helps us keep an eye on things," Jack said.

"Us?" Kristen asked. "Are you speaking of the Masters?"

Cameron stared at her. Was her question out of line?

"Remember the dungeon monitors on Friday night?" Jack asked.

She nodded. "You also keep the music to a low level." Of course, he was talking about the dungeon monitors. Kristen wanted to smack herself for forgetting. "That was nice. You could hear what was going on and have a normal conversation without yelling. Other clubs are not like that."

Jack's eyebrows rose, and he glanced at Cameron.

"She's had some pretty bad experiences," Cameron said quietly, keeping his gaze on Kristen. "It's her story to tell."

Kristen swallowed. There wasn't any reason to hide her experience. "I have," she said, glad her tone was calm and steady. "The place I went to before was not only super dark but had loud music. If there were monitors, they wouldn't have been able to hear anything let alone see if someone was in trouble." A shiver slid up her spine, and she reminded herself that those days were gone. Decadence was a well-run club from what she could see. One she felt safe in with Cameron.

"Well, you don't have to worry about that here," Jack reassured her. "As you noted, we play music, but it's in the background and not overpowering."

"That's a new piece." Cameron guided her two stations down to what looked like a giant, metal spider web attached to a wooden frame.

How had she missed this on Friday? Maybe because after her climax when they'd gone back into the club, her attention had been more focused on Cameron.

"Yes, I love this one." Jack ran his hand over the well-polished wood frame. "It's our newest suspension-bondage piece."

Cameron released her waist and walked over to it. He grabbed the metal web and shook it. "Very nice construction."

"You can bind your sub to the web or use the web for suspension. It also doubles for flogging or whipping."

"Wouldn't the metal hurt the person tied to it?" Kristen tilted her head and stared. It looked awfully uncomfortable. Yet she could see Cameron securing her to the metal, teasing her with his fingers and whispering in her ear, telling her what he was going to do to her. Her pussy tightened.

"Come here." Cameron held his hand out.

Kristen put her hand into his, allowing him to draw

her close.

"Feel the metal." He placed her hand on the crosspiece.

"It's smooth and…almost soft to the touch, but you can feel the strength in it."

"I take player safety very seriously," Jack said.

Cameron leaned close to her and whispered, "I can't wait to see you bound here and my flogger turning your skin pink with excitement."

Kristen shivered with anticipation, but she turned and pointed to another station before she melted into a puddle at Cameron's feet. "That's another one I haven't seen before."

"This one has been very popular," Jack said. "It's a custom-built, modular bondage system."

Kristen looked at the frame which had metal rings at the top, then lots of wooden slats in-between—some with holes, some without. It had a medieval feeling to it.

"Oh, wow." Cameron walked over to the piece of equipment. "Modular bondage system." His tone was hushed as he looked at each piece.

"I don't get it." To her, it just looked like an odd piece of metal and wood to tie someone to.

"Everything moves," Cameron said. "It will allow a Dom to tie and torment a sub in different positions." He looked at Jack. "Do you have pictures? I'd like Kristen to see how it works."

Jack grinned. "Oh yeah, Diane let me take some. Let me go get them." He jogged out of the room.

Cameron smiled.

She laughed and said, "You look like a kid in a candy shop." And for some reason, that made her happy.

"I am. We drooled over this one for months." He returned to her side. "Anything else you need explained?"

Kristen looked around the club. St. Andrew's crosses, bondage chairs and tables—standard stuff she'd seen before. "I'm good." She was better than good; her clit tingled in anticipation of using some of the equipment at a future date.

"Have I scared you?"

Kristen smiled. "No. I like that you and Jack are very conscious of safety. It's not always that way."

"You've had some bad experiences. It's one of the reasons Jack and I work so well together. We believe in education and safety."

Jack walked back into the room and held a small album out to Cameron.

Kristen stood next to Cameron as he opened it, then she gasped. "Oh, dear Lord."

They say pictures are worth a thousand words… But these made all her words disappear. Seeing the pictures of a sub tied up to the bondage system in different positions made all the difference in the world in realizing how the piece worked. The thought of having him use the system on her in a private setting— maybe in a couple of months when she was more secure with Cameron and kink—sent a thrill of anticipation up her spine.

"Those are just a few of the positions you can do. We haven't experimented too much yet. We've only had it a month," Jack explained.

Kristen looked at the bondage system then back at the pictures. They could tie someone up within the frame. There was a bench that could be pulled out and used, and there were stocks...so many ways to bind someone and put them on display.

"Advanced players only?" Cameron asked.

"Yes."

"Excuse me," Piper said from the doorway. "Jack, some of the new members are arriving."

"Duty calls. See you in fifteen in the classroom." Jack loped out of the room.

Kristen kept looking between the pictures and the equipment, trying to equate the two, her mind spinning over how it would feel to be put on display like that.

"Think about it," Cameron whispered in her ear while tapping one of the pictures. "You laying there, your head and arms in the stocks, legs in the calf stirrups, and your ankles restrained. You're wide open to me for whatever I want to do."

Kristen's mouth dropped open; she couldn't get in enough air. She could picture Cameron standing next to her, bent over in the stock, tormenting her with a flogger or just his lips. Her skin tingled, and her pussy tightened. Oh. Dear. God.

"Cameron." Her voice was soft and husky with need.

"One day." He closed the album then drew her into his arms. "One day, when you're ready." He gave her a quick, hard kiss before setting her away from him. "Come on. You have a class to attend."

On shaky legs, she followed him out of the club and into the classroom. This was going to be an interesting afternoon.

****

"Well, what did you think?" Cameron asked later

that afternoon as he pulled out the takeout containers from the bags at his home.

"My head is full." Kristen grinned as she finished setting out silverware on the breakfast bar. He'd gone over a lot of topics. Everything made her more eager to learn and spend time with Cameron.

"Most classes are like that." He waited until she sat down before he took his own seat. "Eat up."

She put some food on her plate before glancing back at him. "I understand Safe, Sane, and Consensual. But RACK…that was new to me."

"Risk Aware Consensual Kink." He loaded his plate with food. "While all of us at the club practice SSC, RACK is just another part."

"But is it unsafe?"

"It can be. The whole thing with RACK is knowing whatever scene you're about to participate in could have some risk."

"Like blood play?" She wanted to understand the difference between SSC and RACK.

"Yes, because sometimes, accidents do happen. Subs need to understand the risk, as do the Doms."

Kristen nodded. That made sense. "The rules of the club are pretty extensive." That had surprised her. She hadn't expected so many rules around play, not after what she'd seen before.

"The rules are there to protect everyone. We do have city, county, and state laws to follow. Thankfully, they are pretty lenient. Jack wanted a place people felt safe to explore their kinkiness and not worry about what other people thought."

"How did you learn about Decadence?" she asked before taking a bite of her food.

"I'd been teaching at the university for about three years when Jack asked if he could audit the class."

"Audit?"

"It's someone who wants to take the class for no credits or a grade."

"Oh." She ducked her head and scrunched up her face. *Stupid question.*

"Kristen." Cameron's voice was sharp. "Look. At. Me." Each word came out firmer than the last one.

She lifted her head to find him staring at her. She fought against hiding behind her hands or running out of the room.

"Remember what I said earlier today. The only stupid question is the unasked one."

Her mouth dropped open. "How did you know?"

"When you're embarrassed, you drop your head down. And there's no need to ever be embarrassed with me."

"I…" She shook her head. She had no idea what to say. Most of her life, her family had belittled her for just about anything. Her grandmother had done her best to keep her confidence up, but it wasn't until she broke away from her family that she had found her independence. But sometimes, she slipped into old patterns. No more. She wanted to do more kinky stuff with Cameron.

Cameron took a sip of water. "Anyway, Jack sat through my class for the semester. After it was over, he approached me, asking me if I was willing to help him get Decadence off the ground."

"Are you his partner in the club?" she asked.

"No. I helped him get the permits, worked with the town council, and helped get everything up and running."

"I'm surprised the town folks here in Grant allowed the club to exist."

"You'd be surprised." Cameron pushed his empty plate away. "There were requirements to get things started. The club had to be on the outskirts of town where traffic and people wouldn't bother anyone."

"It's a nice building. Bigger than I thought it would be."

"Yeah, Jack wanted the club to be unique. The building was a small, abandoned warehouse. He bought it for a song and the sale included the land around it."

"I know Jack owns the gas station, but that must have cost him a pretty penny, even here in Grant." She thought of the cost of her café with the apartment above it. It had taken most of her inheritance from her grandmother to purchase the place.

She closed her eyes, and her shoulders sagged. What would her grandmother think of her now? Would she be upset that Kristen had left California to make her own way? No, she was probably cheering her on from the grave. Granny had always told her to do what she wanted to do, not what she thought everyone wanted her to do. But her parents? They would be horrified.

"You're sad. What happened?" Cameron asked.

Kristen hadn't even noticed the tears in her eyes. "I was just remembering my grandmother." She shook her head and took a deep breath. "It was because of her that I was able to come to Grant and start my business."

"You miss her." He reached across the table and caressed the back of her hand.

"Yes. She was a special woman, regardless of the family she married into." She gave him a half smile.

"We might as well get comfortable."

Cameron slid his chair back and stood, holding his hand out to her. She placed her hand in his. He led her into the family room and stopped in front of the love seat, snagging her around the waist and tumbled them onto it.

She laughed as he wiggled into position with her in his lap. "Is everything so physical with you?"

"Yes." He flashed a quick smile. "I love having you in my arms, feeling your skin beneath mine."

Heat flared in her core and spread out through her body like an out-of-control forest fire. "You make me feel so special."

"You are special." He brushed his lips over her nose. "Will you tell me about your grandmother?"

"Yes." Talking about her grandmother was one thing she could do. She snuggled into his arms. "As I said, Granny was an exceptional woman."

Cameron fingers trail through her hair as she began talking. His touch soothed her, allowing her to talk.

"She always encouraged me to be myself and ignore what the family wanted."

Cameron hid his surprise at her willingness to talk about her family, but he wasn't going to stop her. She was running from something, and maybe he'd finally find out what it was. "How old were you when she died?

"Almost twenty-eight." She wiggled in his lap. "I took care of her for four years before she passed."

"What happened?" The pain in her voice pulled at his heart.

"She'd had some serious health issues. My parents wanted to put her in a home, but I refused to let them do it. So I stepped up to the plate and took on her care."

"Are your parents still living?"

"Yep, and…" She stiffened. "Enough. I don't want to talk about them."

Cameron was careful to keep his frustration to himself, but he wanted to know more. Something about her parents upset her, and he suspected their reaction to kink was part of the issue. He wanted to help her, but he could only do that if she allowed it.

He said, "One day soon, you will tell me the story of your family, Kristen."

She started to pull away.

Cameron put a hand across her lap, not holding her captive, but reminding her that this was a safe place. "I know this is a hard story for you to tell. That's why I have waited for you to want to tell it."

She started to shake her head, then ducked it instead.

Cameron sighed inwardly and pulled her tight, holding her and murmuring until she relaxed against him. He'd bet anything this was the reason Kristen balked at anything public. There was much more to this story, and he would find out.

But it was time to move on to another subject. A more pleasant one. "Tell me a fantasy?"

"What?"

He pressed his hand against her head when she would have lifted it, keeping her cheek against his chest. "I want to know what your sexual fantasies are."

She wiggled in his lap. "Why?"

"So I can make one come true."

Her laughter brushed against his skin, and his muscles unclenched. She was learning to trust him.

"Well, I do have this one. It's a kidnap fantasy."

He listened to her describe her fantasy until her voice drifted off, and she fell asleep in his arms.

"One day," he murmured. "One day soon."

Chapter Fourteen

Kristen yawned as she put the muffins into the oven. It was six fifteen in the morning, and Cameron would be there soon. Her heart jumped at seeing him this morning.

Cameron. He'd been in his element yesterday while teaching at the club. Now she understood why the kids always commented that he was one of the best professors. She had been fascinated with how he made even the rules of the club come alive. He had answered questions, telling everyone it didn't matter what the question was, there was no right or wrong. They were there to learn and become a part of the community. And Kristin was already starting to feel like part of the community.

Then Jack had come in and introduced several of the other workers at the club. She couldn't wait until next week's class. A knock on the front door brought her out of her musings.

She hurried out of the kitchen to see Cameron standing outside. With a grin, she crossed the room and let him in. "Good morning."

He swept her into his arms and covered her lips with his. Her arms went around his neck, and her lips parted to his questing tongue. He tasted like mint, and she liked it. His hands slid down her back and cupped her ass, pulling her tight against him. Lord, she loved being in his arms. He made her feel safe and protected.

She tore her mouth away. "Cameron." She wiggled in his embrace. They were in plain sight of anyone walking by.

"*Now,* it's a good morning." He smiled at her, his eyes twinkling mischievously.

"You're in a good mood." She squirmed out of his arms and made her way behind the counter to make his coffee.

"Yes. My dad stopped by this morning."

"He was up very early."

"Yep. He reminded me about the Grant Highland Games."

Kristen's gaze went to the calendar she had on the wall. "Damn, I totally forgot about it." The Highland Games were a great community event. People came from all over to participate in the games, but there were also lots of vendors. The first year, she had set up a small tent and had sold only cookies, but now, she had a bigger tent and sold a full range of breakfast foods, coffee, tea, water, desserts, cookies and other sweets. It was a big money-maker for her.

"It's in a month, and I'm looking forward to it, especially since we're together."

"Why does that sound…shall we say…naughty?" She slid the cup of coffee across the counter to him.

"Because I have plans."

"That's what I'm afraid of." She let out a laugh. "Scones are warming; let me go get you one." Kristen slipped into the kitchen. She took two scones and put them on a plate, then returned to Cameron, who was sitting at his table by the window.

"Here you go." She set the plate down in front of

him.

"Sit for a moment."

No one was in the café yet, so it was okay. Tim would be here at seven to help out. She sank in the chair across from him. "What's up?"

"I know you always have a dessert tent at the games, but I'd like us to spend some time together, so I can show you around."

"It's one of my biggest selling events." She mentally calculated how much baking she would have to do leading up to the games. It was only one weekend, but a heck of busy weekend. Tim could handle the café on Saturday. Her time with Cameron would be restricted the week before the games, and she wasn't happy with that, but her business came first.

"I'm sure Skye would help." Cameron sipped his coffee.

He's trying to be helpful, Kristen told herself. "Yes, but she's also very busy at the games." This was getting complicated, but only if she let it. She wanted to spend time with Cameron. She could work things out with Skye and Tim.

The bell rang, signaling someone coming into the café. Kristen glanced up to see Tim. She looked up at the clock. It was six forty-five. Dang, time flew when she was with Cameron.

"Morning, boss," Tim called before heading to the back.

Kristen nibbled on her lip. She wanted to see the games with Cameron, but she also had a business to run. "I'll need to think about it."

"Sweetheart." His warm fingers curled around hers. "We have time."

She nodded and pulled her hand away. "I've got work to do, and you have classes to teach." She stood. Her mind whirled with all she had to do for the Highland Games. But also, she thought about being escorted around by Cameron and this time, saw the people staring. What would people think about her and Cameron? Why couldn't she get over her past? It was her problem, always worrying what other people thought, and she needed to stop. Yeah, she had to stop, but it had been drummed into from the time she was little. Sometimes, it was difficult to overcome bad habits.

Cameron rose, but kept his gaze on her. Kristen shifted on her feet as he stared. She was hiding from him, but she didn't know any other way. Hiding was a way to protect herself and her emotions.

He let out a breath. "Think about it. I'll see you later."

The frustration in his voice made her sad. He brushed a kiss over her lips before grabbing his bag and sauntering out the door.

Kristen sighed and picked up his empty plate and coffee cup. How was she going to make this work? Because she had to find a way. She wasn't ready to give Cameron up. Not yet.

****

By the end of the week, Kristen was no closer to a decision about spending time with Cameron at the Highland Games, but the good news was that she had hired two more workers at the café. With Tim's class schedule taking up his time and the increase in business, she needed help.

The new hire, Maggie, was a sociology major in

her senior year. The other hire, Jessica, was a business major but only taking two classes this semester.

The darkening night sky had Kristen locked the café door, turned the lights out and made her way upstairs to her apartment. Both Jessica and Maggie would start their training tomorrow. Skye would be here as well, so maybe things would go smoothly.

She took a quick shower then changed into a light skirt and blouse. Even though it almost the end of March, the weather had turned nice. Cameron would be there any second to pick her up for dinner.

After Monday, he hadn't mentioned the Highland Games again, but it was in the back of her mind, mingling with thoughts about the club and the next class on Sunday.

Cameron had been busy this week with his classes, so they really hadn't had any quality time together, and she missed him. That was a new sensation for her. She slipped on her shoes as a knock sounded at her door.

"Coming." She strode to the door and checked to make sure it was Cameron before opening it.

Cameron stood there with a big grin on his face. "Oh, shall I find a way to have you coming all night?" he asked before sweeping her into his arms for a swift, hard kiss.

"Cameron," she half-heartedly protested. Despite Cameron being busy, they'd texted and talked all week, and she was enjoying his sensual teasing.

He kissed her again; his kisses made her knees grow weak. As his tongue dueled with hers, her nipples tightened.

He lifted his head. "I made us reservations at Rossi's."

"Isn't that the new, fancy Italian place?" She extracted herself from his arms and picked up her purse.

"Yep. I figured it would be a nice change of pace." He guided her out of her apartment and waited while she locked the door, then he took her hand as they walked down the stairs.

After a short car drive through Grant, Cameron escorted her into Rossi's. Rossi's was very nicely decorated. The walls appeared to be covered in stone; the music was low and sensuous. And the lobby was full of people.

Cameron guided her to the hostess station. "Reservation under McMillan."

"Ah yes, Mr. McMillan, I have your table ready for you." The hostess picked up two menus. "If you'll follow me."

Cameron gestured for Kristen to go first. She glanced around as they were escorted to their table. It looked as if half of Grant was here tonight. Well, it was a new restaurant. Everyone wanted to try it out.

"Oh my," she said under her breath as they were led out into a lush courtyard. Free-standing propane lamp heaters were spread throughout the area, keeping the coolness at bay.

The tables were spaced enough apart to give some privacy. The solid-wood tables gleamed, and the tan wicker chairs looked comfortable. Her shoes clicked against what looked like expensive Italian marble flooring, and it accented the table and chairs. A huge oak tree rose from the middle of the courtyard.

As the hostess led them to a table, Kristen felt it was like a "who's who" night out. The mayor and his wife nodded to them as they walked by, and then Mrs.

Johnson waved her fork at them as her husband continued to eat. And if she wasn't mistaken, that was Skye with Malcolm McCray. *So that's why Skye was in a hurry to leave tonight.*

Cameron waved to his sister before pulling out Kristen's chair. She took her seat and tucked her purse between her thigh and the chair. She was surprised at how roomy the seats were.

"Your waiter will be here in a few minutes. Have a fantastic dinner," the hostess said after setting the menus down.

Cameron had taken a seat to Kristen's right, and he had a full view of the room. Kristen, had a partial view of the room, but it felt like everyone was starting at her. *I know what you've been doing...* She clenched her hands in her lap, trying not to let her discomfort show. It seemed like every time she and Cameron were together, she managed to ruin the mood.

"What has you frowning?" Cameron slid the menus aside and placed his hand palm up on the table.

"Was I?" She fought to clear her expression.

"Kristen." Cameron's voice went to that low, Dom tone she associated with the times they'd played. He tapped his fingers on the table before turning his palm up.

Her fingers trembled when she placed them over his. His skin was hot against her cold digits.

"What is it?" Now a frown marred his forehead.

"It's fine."

His fingers tightened on her hand. "It's not. You're trembling and cold. Should I have them move us inside?"

"No." She glanced up at the clear, star filled sky.

"It's a beautiful night." Her trembling had nothing to do with cold.

"Then tell me what's wrong?"

She opened her mouth, but Cameron narrowed his eyes. She swallowed the words she was about to say. He wasn't going to let her hide.

"It's really nothing." How could she explain?

Cameron scooted closer to her, sitting there silently until she looked at him. "Tell. Me. Now."

A shiver snaked up her spine. Not in apprehension, but in excitement. When he used that tone, her bones all melted. She let out a sigh. "I feel like I'm on display."

"Is that why you think I brought you here?"

"No," she whispered. "It's just…" She closed her eyes then opened them. "Everyone is here tonight, and it brings up old fears."

The waiter walked up. "Good evening, I'm David, your waiter for this evening."

Cameron turned his attention to the waiter, but tightened his grip on her hand when she would have pulled away. "Evening, David."

"Would you like a wine list?"

Kristen looked at their waiter. He didn't look old enough to serve alcohol. His shaggy but well-kept sandy-blond hair made her think of him as a surfer.

"No need. A bottle of 1996 Barolo," Cameron said.

"Very good choice. Appetizer?"

"Yes, an order of the cheese and spinach puffs."

Kristen stared at Cameron. Had he been here before?

"Have you decided on dinner?"

"Yes." Cameron squeezed her hand. "I'll have the shrimp scampi with linguini, and my lady here will have the shrimp risotto."

"Soups or salad?"

"Minestrone soup and some water, please."

"Very good, sir." The waiter picked up the menus. "I'll have the wine steward bring over your Barolo."

Kristen waited until the waiter was out of ear shot. "What was that? You've never ordered for me without asking."

"Tonight, you will allow me to take care of you."

"Cameron."

His fingers covered her lips. "For one night, Kristen. You've had a long week. We both have. Let me do this for you."

Her heart stopped, partly in worry and fascination. His features were soft but his gaze intense. Was this a test? It could be, but she didn't think so. This was his way of showing her he cared. She nodded, and his grip relaxed on her hand.

"Now tell me why you're worried about everyone seeing you here tonight?" He kept his gaze on her.

"It, umm, relates back to the ex-fiancé." She tugged her hand free, only to caress his wrist. "You're nothing like him, but he would take me out to show me off." Just like her parents had.

"I wouldn't do that to you."

"I know that here." She touched her head. "But sometimes, the heart doesn't realize it." Her fingers drifted over his the skin of his hand, stroking, caressing. "My parents would always drag me out, too, to show off the perfect little family." She winced at the bitterness in her voice.

"Tell me." His attention was centered on her, and Kristen took a deep breath.

"They took me out anytime they wanted to project the aura of loving parents, to keep themselves in the limelight. They didn't care what it did to me. If I had so much as a hair out of place or a wrinkle in my clothes, the ridicule would start."

"Not exactly loving parents to chastise you in public."

"Oh, it wasn't always from them, but from everyone else." She stomach clenched as the comments about her looks, her actions—anything was always public fodder.

"What?" He shook his head.

"Appearance was everything in that circle, and I was expected to conform. If I didn't, everyone let me know about it."

"Kristen, that was never my intention."

Her fingers pressed against his lips. "I know it wasn't. Everyone in Grant is nice. But that doesn't mean they won't judge me on my actions or lifestyle." She let her fingers slide from his lips.

"No one should judge someone else. We're all human." He captured her hand and kissed her knuckles.

"Yeah, tell my parents that."

Cameron didn't know how to respond. The ex and her parents had wounded her deeper than Cameron had realized. He wouldn't say what he wanted to—her parents were idiots—at least, not now. His parents were loving, caring, and thoughtful.

He stood up and moved behind her chair. With a quick adjustment, he maneuvered Kristen's chair around and closer to his so she could see the room and know they weren't being watched or judged. "There. That should help you put your fears aside to enjoy tonight?" He hoped she could, because he wanted to pamper her. "Besides, I'm going to make you forget there's even anyone else here."

The wine steward walked up. "Sir, your bottle of 1996 Barolo."

Cameron nodded as the steward poured a small amount of the red wine in a glass and then handed it to him.

His gaze captured Kristen's as he swirled the wine. He took a small sip then held the glass up to her lips. "Taste." He tilted the glass up, and she sipped.

"Wow," she said as he lowered the glass. "Full bodied and a hint of spice."

"It's perfect." He handed the glass back to the waiter. Cameron waited until the wine was poured and for the steward to leave, then he picked up the glasses and handed her one. "May tonight be filled with laughter, fun, and naughtiness."

They touched their glasses and drank. She had talked to him tonight, told him more about her family. She was trying. Maybe this was a turning point in their relationship. Maybe not going to Scotland was a good idea.

Chapter Fifteen

"Dinner was delicious," Kristen said as Cameron drove toward his house. Once she had relaxed, Cameron had showed her how he cared for her. He'd taken the appetizer and fed the puffs to her from his fingers. At first she was self-conscious that it would call attention to them, but no one paid them any mind.

Even though they were in public, it was magical. He also made sure her soup had the right about of cheese on top, and he had even fed her part of his scampi, laughing when she'd insisted on feeding him some of her risotto. This night was special.

After he parked, she slipped from his SUV and stared up at the night sky. Stars twinkled against a black canvas. A peacefulness swept over her, one she hadn't felt in a very long time.

"Would you like to sit on the back porch for a while?" Cameron asked.

"That would be nice." It was warm enough, and she didn't want the evening to end yet. She wanted to be with Cameron.

He guided her around to the back of his house. The porch was wood, and in the distance, she could make out trees. Light illuminated a path, and there were some plants lining it. She inhaled and the scents of pine, jasmine and carnations made her smile.

She turned. "Oh, you have a porch swing. How did

165

I miss that?"

"Well, it could be because I never brought you back here." He grinned at her. "Sit down and get comfortable. Would you like some more wine?"

"Yes, please."

He unlocked the back door and slip inside. Instead of sitting, Kristen stood at the edge of the porch, just staring out at the stars. The night was so beautiful and quiet.

Well, maybe not so quiet because the crickets were chirping, but she wouldn't trade this for anything. She turned, went over to the swing, and sat down. The swing had a high back so she could lean her head back and...oh, wow. The canopy was tilted in such a way she could still see the night sky.

"Your wine, my lady."

"Thanks." She took the glass Cameron held out to her and took a sip of the white wine. "This is wonderful."

"It's a nice Riesling." He took her glass and set it on the small side table, then knelt at her feet. "Let's get you comfortable." Before she could say a word, he slipped off her shoes. Then, he sat next to her and maneuvered her body so her head was on his lap.

She gazed up at Cameron's handsome, rugged face and wondered how she got so lucky to have him in her life.

"What are you thinking?" he asked. "Your eyes are glowing."

Kristen couldn't help but smile. "I was thinking what a wonderful man you are."

"Flattery."

"Truth." She covered his hand where it rested on

her stomach. "How is it you're not married?"

A slight shadow spread over his features then disappeared. "I've never found a woman I wanted to spend my life with." He brushed her hair away from her forehead before trailing a fingertip from her temple down her cheek.

His touch was soft and sensuous. She wanted more. While they'd played together, tonight was different. Maybe it was time to open up more to him. "After my grandmother died, you know I came here to Grant."

"How did you pick Grant?" His hand dropped to her shoulder.

She laughed. "I actually got in my car and just started driving."

"That sounds impulsive and dangerous."

"At the time I just wanted to get away." She blinked away the tears filling her eyes. "I packed up what I could, hit the lawyer's office, and took off."

"Your family never looked for you?"

She sat up and faced Cameron. If she was going to confess this, she wanted to see his face, his reaction. "I legally changed my last name when I came to Grant."

Cameron blinked, but his expression didn't change. No disapproval lingered there. "Why?"

"Because I didn't want to be found," she whispered. "I hated my life, hated I had become—a lifeless doll. I wanted a fresh start." Tears filled her eyes. "I'd buried my grandmother, and all my parents could talk about was how to milk it with the press."

"Sweetheart." He cupped her chin in his palm. "I love you are opening up to me, but I hate to see you so upset. I can't take it." His lips brushed hers.

Her heart clenched at Cameron's words. He was so

caring and concerned. She was falling for this man. Kristen inhaled. Yes, she was falling for Cameron; it was more than kink. She decided then and there, she would see this to the end whatever it maybe.

She shifted to kiss him and the swing tilted. She squeaked in fear of falling onto the porch.

Cameron's arms curled around her waist. "Why don't we take this inside?"

"Yes, inside," she whispered then looked him in the eye. "To your bedroom."

His blue eyes darkened. Without a word, he stood and scooped her up into his arms. After locking the back door, his long, firm strides carried them up the stairs to his room.

Kristen's heart sped up. She wanted him. She wanted to be close to him, to feel his love embrace her entire being.

When Cameron set her on her feet, she got her first good look at his bedroom—dark with little decorating flair. A laugh escaped her lips.

"What is that laugh for?" he asked.

"Typical, male bedroom." She waved her hand at the large, wood-framed bed. The heavy, old-looking oak dresser, dark and looming, made her bite her lip. What stories could that dresser could tell? An overstuffed chair with a side table overflowing with books and magazines caused her to grin; at least he was a reader. There was a multi-colored throw rug that helped make the room look less dark. A large, flat-screen TV was mounted on the wall, and dark curtains were pulled closed over the windows.

"I like it." He tugged her into his arms again. "Besides, what better place to ravish you?"

"Oh, so you're going to ravish me?"

"And then some." He grinned. "I'm in charge."

"Yes, Sir." Damn if her blood didn't heat up in her veins. She loved it when he took control, allowing her to throw her thoughts away and concentrate only on pleasure.

"Very good. Now, it's time for me to unwrap my present."

His lips brushed against hers. Kristen opened her mouth to his, her tongue finding his, toying with it before he took control.

She sank against his body. Heat filled her body, and her breathing hitched. Lord, the man could kiss. All too soon, he pulled away.

His fingers found the hem of her shirt, and in a swift move, he whisked it up and over her head. Her skin pebbled in the cool air, but she wasn't cold. She was hot. Very hot.

Her hard nipples pressed against her lace bra. Cameron lowered his head, his lips trailing over her collar bone. "So beautiful."

The next thing she knew, her bra was off, and Cameron kissed his way to her stomach. He stopped and gazed up at her as he unfastened her skirt, pushing it and her lacy panties to the floor. Kristen's breath hitched in her throat as he stood.

"Undress me," he commanded.

For some reason, her fingers shook as she undid his shirt, pushing it off his shoulders to fall to the floor. She ran her nails over his chest, following the trail of chest hair until it disappeared beneath his trousers.

She bit her lower lip. She'd never been asked to strip a man before, but how hard could it be? Her fingers closed over his belt, loosened it, and pulled it from the loops.

The leather belt hung heavy in her hands. She let it slip from her fingers, the buckle clanking on the floor. With deft movements, she unfastened his pants and pushed them down.

"Commando," she whispered as the fabric gave way to the dark curls nestled at the base of his very erect cock.

"Always." He drew her to a standing position. "Get on the bed. Now."

His deep, husky voice sent shivers of anticipation through her. She padded over to the bed and drew back the dark brown comforter to reveal tan sheets. Grabbing the top sheet, she pushed it down to the end of the bed as well.

"You keep shaking that perky ass at me, and I'm going to enjoy spanking it."

Hot tendrils of desire climbed her spine. Kristen glanced over her shoulder and fluttered her lashes before climbing onto the mattress with one last shake of her ass. She barely had one knee on the bed when she was tackled from behind.

"You asked for it." Cameron's hand pressed against the middle of her back, keeping her upper half on the bed but allowing her legs to dangle over the side. He brought his hand down on her ass.

Heat flared in her ass. A little bit of pain blended into pleasure. He raised his palm and repeated the action. He wasn't hitting her hard, and he didn't hit in the same place twice, moving around her backside to heat her flesh. Each strike sent her closer to climax, higher and higher. Her clit throbbed, her nipples pulsed, and her pussy clenched. The strikes stopped, and his palm caressed her hot skin.

"More. Please, Sir." At least she remembered to call him Sir.

"Not tonight." His hands lifted her at the waist and slid her fully onto the mattress.

Kristen turned her head. His cock was fully erect and weeping. She reached out and spread his wetness around his red-looking cock head before bringing her finger to her mouth. Salty, but all Cameron.

"Witch." He placed a knee on the bed.

She turned onto her back and slid farther up the mattress.

"Oh, no." He captured her ankles and pulled her back. "My turn."

Before she could ask him what he meant, he hefted her legs onto his shoulders.

"Cameron."

His mouth closed over her clit, his tongue flicking it. *Oh Lord.* Wetness seeped from her pussy as he licked and sucked. He tormented her with each pass until she was writhing on the bed.

His head rose. "You taste so sweet." Then he dove back into his work.

Her body was on fire under the sweet torment of his tongue and lips. Her stomach tightened; she was close, so very close. Her fingers curled into her palms. It wasn't going to take much more before she climaxed.

Before she could take another breath, Cameron plunged two fingers into her core. She cried out as she clenched around the digits. Her mouth dropped open as hot flames of pleasure shot through her pussy, to her clit, and back. He pumped his fingers in and out of her while tormenting her clit, drawing her climax out.

When her climax finally subsided to mild tremors, Cameron lifted his head and smiled at her. "Sweet as cotton candy." He lifted her legs from his shoulders and settled them around his hips.

"I..." She had no words. She'd never come that hard. Even when they had played together, her arousal had been there, but it had never ended a climax like this one.

"There's more."

She blinked. "More, Sir?" she whispered.

He leaned down and kissed his way up her stomach to her breasts. Cameron paused there, taking one nipple in his mouth and playing with it until it was so hard she thought it would burst. Then he proceeded to do the same thing with the other one.

Tingles flowed over her skin. A sense of satisfaction mingled with anticipation. When would he let her taste him? Her mouth watered at the idea of taking his hard cock into her mouth and bringing him to climax.

Her neck arched as he nibbled her skin along her jaw, his mouth creating shivers of delight to play over her body. Her legs tightened around his waist.

"Soon," he whispered against her skin. His lips covered hers, and their tongues tangled. A tangy flavor hit her senses, and she pulled back in surprise at tasting herself on his lips.

Cameron rested his forehead against hers. "So sweet, so spicy. So you." His lips found hers again.

Kristen's arms slid around his back, nails tracing his skin lightly. She was so ready for him. Her hips wiggled. It was a good thing they'd discussed birth control in the beginning, because she couldn't wait until his hard dick was driving into her.

He shifted his lower body, keeping her legs around his waist as his cock brushed her entrance. She lifted her hips.

His mouth left hers. "No moving."

"What?" He had to be kidding.

"My rules. Stay still, or I will punish you." He pushed farther inside her pulsing pussy.

She let out a groan and forced her hips to remain still. "You're going to kill me, Sir."

"Never." His lips covered hers again as he thrust hard.

Her muscles clenched then released as he lunged inside her pussy. Pure heaven. His cock was so hard, making her pussy spasm with desire and need. Her eyes closed, and she tore her mouth from his, puffing out a breath, fighting the urge to move. "So big, Sir."

"Perfect for you." His voice was strained.

He drew back and thrust forward. Her pussy tightened around him, trying to pull him in deeper. "More, Sir," she whispered.

"You are so beautiful," he said as he shifted within her. "Your skin flushed, your body quivering with need, your pussy clamping down on my dick."

His words took her need higher. "You're so hard, Sir."

"For you. Only for you."

He plunged into her, and she let out a moan as he ground against her clit. Kristen tried to catch her breath. Damn, she wanted to move, but she'd make him proud of her. "So full."

Without a condom, every inch of his cock rubbed

the delicate interior of her pussy. Sweet, delicious pleasure pulsed from her core, to her stomach, traveling to her nipples, making them throb with need. Her clit throbbed and shivers of pleasure across her skin. She couldn't catch her breath as her pussy muscle clenched around his shaft, wanting more.

"Are you ready?"

She opened her eyes and gazed into his deep blue ones. "For what, Sir?"

"This."

He glided out of her pussy and then dove back into her—hard. Her mouth dropped open, and her neck arched as he did it again. Each time, he thrust harder and faster. Her fingers dug into his back as he pistoned in and out of her. Her muscles tightened around his cock, not wanting to let it slide away.

"I love how you grasp my dick, making me want to fuck you even harder."

His words inflamed her already overheated senses. "I…"

Her body shook as her climax unexpectedly took over. She arched her neck holding back her cries of pleasure, while fighting to maintain control. Oh, who was she kidding? She had no control with him.

"That's it, baby. Come for me. Show me your pleasure."

"Cameron," she cried as he rotated his hips, putting pressure against her clit. Tremors began building again as he continued to take her higher and higher.

"Come again, sweetheart." His hot breath brushed against her ear.

She shook her head. Wasn't two enough? But it seemed like her body had other ideas, as did Cameron.

The harder he plunged, the more her core tightened, until…her nails dug into his back, and she screamed out her orgasm.

"So fucking beautiful."

His words barely penetrated the intense pleasure coursing through her body, shaking her to the core.

"My turn." The words were spoken against her mouth as his lips captured hers. With a hard push, he stilled. His cock pulsed inside her pussy, wringing another mini-orgasm from her.

He released her mouth, and their heavy breathing filled the room. Her clit throbbed, and her pussy clenched around his cock as if it wanted more.

Somehow, Cameron managed to keep his full weight off of her. She ran her palms over his sweaty back, enjoying the idea that she could do this to him.

When he started to pull back, she tightened her arms around him. "No, Sir" she whispered.

"I don't want to crush you." He shifted, and her legs fell from around his hips. He rolled them onto their sides, keeping her snuggled in his arms.

"So good. Don't want it to end," she murmured, her lashes falling. She didn't want to move. She was so sated, so satisfied. She'd think about going home later. "Sir."

Chapter Sixteen

Skye yawned as she walked into the café's kitchen the next morning at seven thirty.

"Late night?" Kristen asked, pushing a tray of muffins into the oven and stifling her own yawn.

She'd woken in Cameron's arms around one in the morning before he curled his big body around hers, telling her to go back to sleep. He'd have her home by five thirty. And he had, dropping her off with a grin, telling her he was going home to prep their scene today, but he refused to tell her where the scene would take place. The thought of a scene sent her world spinning out of control.

"Probably as late as yours was." Skye put her purse away and slipped on her apron.

"Maybe." She followed Skye out into the café. "Coffee is ready. No big orders today. Ordered cakes are in the fridge and marked. Everything for this morning is made or can easily be put in the oven." She'd managed to get everything ready in record time.

"I've got it covered, boss. Why don't you go get ready for your day with Cameron?"

"It's only…" She looked up at the clock—eight. How had that happened? It was time to open up.

A knock sounded on the glass door, and Kristen looked up to see the man himself standing there. Skye let him in and turned the "open" sign on.

"Do I need to talk to McCray?" Cameron asked, tilting his sister's face up so he could look into her eyes.

"I don't need the big brother routine; it was just a friendly date," Skye retorted.

"How friendly?"

Kristen burst out laughing, and the pair turned toward her.

"Probably no more friendly than our date last night." Heat filled her when she realized what she'd said out loud. Thank goodness, it was just the three of them.

"That's what I'm afraid of." He sauntered over to Kristen with a bag in his hand. "Are you ready for our day?"

"More than ready." Today, she hoped to explore more of Cameron's playroom, but the man wouldn't tell her what he had planned.

"Go, you two, before I have to bring out the fire hose." Skye shooed them with her hands. "And don't forget dinner at the house tonight, Cameron. Dad wants to go over everything for next weekend."

"We'll be there."

Kristen tensed, for a minute and then relaxed. Unlike her family dinners where everyone sat in tense silence as they ate, dinner with his family was fun.

Cameron slipped his arm around her waist and escorted her through the kitchen and up to her apartment.

"What's in the bag?" she asked as they entered the living room.

"Never mind that right now." He set the bag by her sofa and drew her into his arms. "I want a kiss." He bent his head.

His lips were cool, but she didn't care. She opened her lips to his questing tongue and tangled hers with his.

When he lifted his head, she smiled at him. "So what's the scene for today?"

"Let's sit down for a minute." He guided her over to the sofa and drew her onto his lap.

"Is there a problem?" Something in the way his muscles tensed up made her wonder. Oh hell, had last night not been as good for him as it had been for her?

"No." He brushed his lips over her cheek. "I want to make sure you're ready for the scene today."

"I'm more than ready." After four weeks of classes at the club and making love last night, her body craved the connection with him. To be his.

"Today, I'm going to take one of your fantasies and make it come true."

"Which one?" Her mind went back to the night they spent curled up on her sofa, discussing their fantasies. Well, mainly hers. She'd told him several of her fantasies.

"If I told you which one, it wouldn't be a surprise." He cupped her chin. "I know your limits, and I will push them a bit. But your safewords still apply."

"'Bacon' to stop, 'cheese' to slow down."

"Yes. I want you to understand this is all for you. I would never hurt you or allow you to be harmed."

"I know that." She kissed his chin. He was the most thoughtful man she'd ever been around. A man who'd wormed his way past the wall she'd built and to be part of her life. Her heart sped up. Cameron had gotten past her defenses, and while it should scare her to death, it didn't. Her breath caught in the realization that he was the first man to accept her for the woman she was.

"Good. So what I want you to do now is go put on these clothes." He handed her the bag he'd set on the floor next to the sofa.

"Okay." She took the bag from him, slid off his lap, and danced into her bedroom. Once there, she emptied the bag onto her bed.

She stared at the black push up bra, the black thong, and the mesh, see-through, black dress. If could be called a dress. It would barely reach the top of her thighs. No stockings, but there was a pair of black shoes with two-inch heels, thank goodness. Anything higher and she'd break her neck. "You've got to be kidding me," she yelled.

"Nope. Put it on, my little subbie."

Damn. He had that tone, one she'd better obey if she didn't want her ass warmed. She let out a giggle. Maybe getting her ass hot wasn't such a bad idea, but not right now. It was still a little tender from last night's spanking.

Kristen dressed, slipped the shoes on, and walked back into her living room. "I can't go out like this, I'll get arrested."

"You look delicious." Cameron stood and strode over to her. "And I don't plan on letting you get arrested. Let me run down to my car. I have a coat for you." He dropped a kiss on her nose before jogging out the front door and down the stairs.

Kristen walked over to the full-length mirror and stared at herself. Yes, she enjoyed dressing up for Cameron, but this was different. Her eyes were bright with desire, and the outfit did make her look sexy. Her legs looked like they went on for miles. Her breasts were full, her nipples poking at the material of the bra. Hell, the thong barely covered the basics. She turned and looked over her shoulder. Oh yeah, her ass was fully on view. Who was this siren?

"You are gorgeous." Cameron came back into the room with a trench coat draped over his arm.

"Thank you." She gave a little curtsy.

Cameron held out the coat, and Kristen slipped her arms into it.

"Let's go."

Kristen took her time going down the stairs. The last thing she wanted to do was fall and break her neck. Cameron held the door open while she sat down, but he waited until she buckled her seat belt.

"Remember that you trust me."

She opened her mouth, but the words died on her lips when she saw the black blindfold dangling from his finger. "I do trust you." She swallowed.

He hadn't blindfolded her before. Unease slipped through her body, and she put her hand up. "Cheese."

Cameron froze. "What is it, sweetheart?"

"I…" She swallowed. "What if someone sees us?"

"It's early enough in the morning. Besides, I'll take the side roads to my house. I want you to open your other senses. I will always protect you. Remember, this is your fantasy, and we've talked about it. Ready?"

She nodded. Her fear subsided a bit. She would try for Cameron, for herself.

"If anything starts to bother you, use your safewords."

The fabric covered her eyes, and within seconds no light penetrated. She took a shaky breath, and when the car door closed, she jumped. *It's okay,* she repeated in her head. The driver's door opened, shut, and the engine started.

"Where are we going?" The vehicle turned left instead of right in the direction of his home.

"Back roads, remember? And you'll see soon enough."

"A little hard with a blindfold on." She gave a giggle.

"You're being a smart-ass, subbie."

"Sorry, Sir." But she wasn't. Without her sight, it was hard to tell where they were going and how long they'd been driving.

"Shit," Cameron said just as the sound of a siren reached her ears.

A cop. "Cameron?"

"It's okay." The car slowed and then stopped. "I'll go talk with the officer. It's probably nothing." The engine turned off, then Cameron opened the car door and closed it.

Kristen sat perfectly still. If the police officer came to the car, he'd see her blindfolded. This was no good, but she trusted Cameron to protect her. Yet a tiny shiver of fear slid up her spine.

Chapter Seventeen

Cameron strode to the car parked behind his in the small outlet just a few miles from his home. "Where did you get the siren?" he asked Jack. Jack was the only one he trusted to help him pull this off, and he was someone who Kristen wouldn't freak out over when she found out who it was.

"Borrowed it from a friend." Jack leaned against the hood of his SUV.

Cameron nodded. They weren't far from his house. He was parked in a small outlet, and he'd already cleared it with the Grant PD that his vehicle would be parked there for a few hours.

"Ready to do this?" Jack asked.

"Yes. I don't think she'll recognize your voice, but you might want to disguise it a bit."

"No problem."

"Remember her safewords are 'cheese' and 'bacon.'"

Jack chuckled. "Who could forget those? I'll go get your lady."

Cameron nodded. Jack sauntered up to Kristen's side of the car and opened her door. Kristen jerked her head toward the open door. Cameron couldn't hear what Jack said as he bent down to her, but Kristen's shoulders stiffened. Jack reached in and undid her seat belt before helping her out of the car. Jealousy rose up within Cameron when Jack held Kristen against him. With a deep breath, he tamped it down. This was her fantasy.

Kristen's movements were jerky as Jack marched her back to his SUV. "Don't make me cuff you." Jack's voice was low and tight.

"No, officer." Kristen's voice was soft, but the slight tremor in it had Cameron frowning. He didn't want her freaking out. He took her in from head to toe. Okay, her body was flushed but not trembling. He chalked her shaky voice to nervousness.

"I don't know what you two are up to, but I will find out." Jack led her to the SUV and opened the back door. "Now, let me help you in."

When Jack touched her ass through the coat to lift her into the vehicle, Kristen let out a squeal and danced away.

"Now, ma'am, calm down."

"Please, just direct me. I can get in myself," Kristen said.

"I don't think so, ma'am, not with that blindfold on."

"Then remove it." Her tone was sharp as her hands rose.

Jack frowned, and Cameron stifled a laugh. Nervous or not, she was a handful.

"I don't think so." Jack captured her wrists and spun her around. "I think it's time for those cuffs." He pressed her against the side of the SUV and expertly cuffed her hands behind her back.

Cameron took a step before he could stop himself. How dare Jack touch her like that? Jack had his body pressed against hers.

Jack stared at him. Cameron shook his head to clear away the jealous rage invading his mind. Jack wasn't interested in Kristen, not in that way. They'd planned this, he reminded himself.

"What have we done? We were just driving. Stop this." Kristen shifted from one foot to the other, trying to escape Jack, but that wasn't about to happen.

Cameron grinned. Oh, what fun they were going to have today. She didn't realize this was her fantasy, did she? Maybe not. Adrenaline could cause interesting reactions.

"Behave." Jack slapped her lightly on her ass.

Kristen stilled immediately. Her mouth dropped open in shock. Before she could recover, Jack lifted her into his arms and put her into the vehicle, clipping the seat belt around her. From his position he was able to see the trench coat parted a bit showing her bare calves.

"So very nice," Jack whispered as Cameron strode quickly to the other side of the SUV and opened the door.

Kristen whimpered.

Cameron frowned. "It's okay, Kristen," Cameron whispered, climbing in.

"Cameron?" She turned her head in his direction.

"I'm here." He leaned over and brushed her lips with his. "It will be okay."

"Don't bet on it," Jack said, then winked at Cameron before slamming the door.

"Cameron, what the hell is going on?" Kristen whispered.

"He said I was speeding."

"You never speed." She squirmed. "Are you cuffed, too?"

"Yes," he lied. There was no way he would allow himself to be restrained when her safety was at stake. He wanted to be able to protect her if something happened when Jack was driving.

"I'm scared." Her voice trembled.

Cameron leaned over. "All will be fine. I'm here, and no one will hurt you as long as I'm alive." She turned her face toward his and their lips brushed.

The sound of Jack closing the driver's door had Kristen pulling away. Cameron nodded at Jack, who started the SUV and drove. Within a few minutes they were at the club.

Cameron wondered when she'd remember her fantasy about being kidnapped and her captor having his way with her. He'd added Jack. He'd worked it out with Jack to allow him to use the club for this. It was safer than trying to take her to his house and risk Kristen figuring out where they were.

"Where are we?" Kristen asked as the vehicle stopped, and Jack turned off the engine.

"I have no idea."

"We're not at the police station?" Her voice was a little high.

"Not that I can see."

Just then, Jack pulled open Cameron's door. "Time to get out."

"Where are we?" Cameron asked.

"None of your business," Jack answered.

Cameron already had his seat belt off. He jumped out, and the door was slammed shut. Jack grinned at Cameron as they moved to the other passenger door. Jack opened the door, reached in, and undid Kristen's seat belt. He lifted her out of her seat

"No, don't move, sweetheart," Cameron said.

Jack slammed the door, and Kristen winced. "You'll both be fine. Just stay with me," Jack said, grasping Kristen's arm as he began walking.

Cameron followed as Jack led a blindfolded Kristen into the club. He locked the front door then went into the dungeon.

Kristen stood before the bondage chair, shivering with what Cameron hoped was excitement. He moved to her side, brushing her arm with his.

"Now, how about an explanation as to why this woman is blindfolded and wearing a trench coat?" Jack's voice was low and hard.

"We…" Kristen stammered. "We were on the way to his house."

"Then why are you blindfolded?"

Kristen turned her head in his direction, and Cameron grinned. "Well, officer," he said, keeping to his role for the moment. "We're into kink."

"Cameron!"

"I have to be truthful, honey. This way, the officer will know we mean no harm."

"Kink, huh." Jack began to circle them. "And what do you have on underneath that coat?" Jack ran his fingers over Kristen's cheek. She flinched away and a sob caught in her throat.

Jack backed away and looked at Cameron.

"Kristen, sweetheart." Cameron put his mouth next to her ear.

"I'm scared," she whispered.

"I know, but remember what I said earlier?"

She shook her head.

"Safewords. Use them if you need them."

She sucked in a breath. "Oh my God." Her chin dropped to her chest as she tried to control her breathing. "Cheese, Sir."

Jack fished the handcuff keys out of his pocket and released her wrists.

"I totally forgot this was one of my fantasies." Her breathing was calmer now, and she was no longer shaking like a leaf.

"We've only slowed down, not stopped." Cameron reminded her as he unbuttoned her coat.

"We?" she squeaked out.

Jack laughed. "Did you really think I was gone?" The fabric parted, and Jack let out a wolf whistle. "Damn that's one fine body."

"Sir?"

"Right here." Cameron slid the coat from her shoulders and laid it over the back of the chair. Part of him wanted to throw Jack out of the room after that wolf whistle, but he fought it away. Jack was his friend and this was a scene. Jack wouldn't touch without permission.

Jack put his hands on her shoulders. "I'm going to lead you over and have you sit down."

"Yes, Sir." Her voice was a little shaky, but she was now aware everything was just part of the scene. Part of her fantasy.

Jack led her over to the bondage chair. "I think we can get rid of this." She started to raise her hands as Jack ripped the mesh dress off her body.

"Oh no, you don't." Jack spun her around and pushed her down onto the seat. He prodded her knees open with his legs and grabbed her wrists. Within seconds, he had her arms spread out against the wood of the bondage chair and restrained.

"Sweetheart, how are you doing?" Cameron asked.

"Green, Sir." Her voice was still a little unsteady, but a small grin played against her lips. "Let me go, you creep. How dare you assault me?" She tugged at her well-secured hands.

"Creep?" Jack ran his fingertips over her shoulders to her throat.

Kristen stiffened.

Jack didn't linger. Instead, he continued his journey, tracing the tops of her breasts where they spilled out of the bra. "Full tits. I like that." He cupped them, running his thumbs over her nipples.

Her mouth opened into an O. Then she shook her head. "Stop it. Cameron, where are you?"

"Right here, my sweet." She was perfect.

"He can't do anything to help you," Jack said. "He's still cuffed."

Kristen struggled again, but she was putting on a show from the smile on her lips. "I don't know who you are, but you'll pay."

"Oh, I will?" Jack's fingers skimmed down to her inner thighs. Using his palms, he pressed them outward until they were spread wide, then he cuffed her thighs and ankles. "I believe I have the upper hand." He slapped the inside of her thighs.

Kristen let out a screech and struggled but not too hard. Jack slapped the inside of her thighs again. With a big grin on his face, Jack sauntered over to Cameron.

"She's perfect, Cam." Jack touched his shoulder. "Two hours. I'll be in my office."

"Thanks, buddy."

Jack ambled from the dungeon. Cameron slipped

off his shirt and shoes before padding over to Kristen.

Kristen's chest shook with each breath she took. Her head swiveled back and forth, trying to figure out what where Cameron was. He was a sneaky man. She'd been so frightened when they'd been pulled over and put in the back of the police vehicle. When he reminded her about her fantasy, she finally had been able to breathe without fear.

"So sweet," Cameron whispered, keeping his voice deep to confuse her. "I can't wait to play with those nipples and that pretty pink pussy I see, peeking out behind the thong."

"Let me go." She wiggled again in her bonds. She was going to make a good show of this.

"You're mine, sweetheart. Mine to play with, mine to enjoy, mine to keep." Cameron's voice wavered as if he turned away from her. "First things first."

Cold metal touched her shoulder. Her bra strap loosened and then fell. Then his fingers were at her back. He undid the fastening, and the fabric fell away.

Her nipples grew harder in the cool room, and her skin grew warm. She was getting turned on. "You blush so nicely and these pretty, rosy nipples." He tweaked one between his thumb and forefinger.

"Ohhh." Her breath left her in a rush as arousal filled her body.

"You like that?"

"No, I don't. You pervert." *Remember to play your part.*

"Ah, watch your mouth." He playfully slapped her breast.

"Ouch," she cried out, but he hadn't hit her hard enough to hurt her, just to sting.

"I have to taste you." He bent down and drew one nipple into his mouth.

She squirmed in her bonds. He playfully bit down on the nub before moving to her other breast and giving it the same treatment. When he was done, her breathing was choppy, and all her nerves were alive, waiting for more.

"Are you ready for more?" he asked, not bothering to disguise his voice this time.

"Yes, Sir." Kristen couldn't wait to find out what Cameron was going to do to her. At the beginning, fear had overwhelmed her. It wasn't until Cameron had talked to her about this morning and about her safewords that she remembered her fantasy. A kidnapping fantasy.

Once her fear had receded, she'd relaxed into the scene and put up mock struggles. She wondered who the other guy was, because she knew it wasn't Cameron. Cameron's touch was softer, more sure of himself. The other person had been hesitant and his skin rougher than Cameron's.

A shiver ran up her spine as Cameron's fingers curved around her hips. Cold metal against her skin had her sucking in a breath. With a swish of metal scissors, her thong was cut from her body.

Now, she was naked before him. Okay, she needed to make this good. "Oh no, please, Sir." She wiggled her legs as if trying to get out of her bonds. The cool air caressed her pussy, making it tingle.

"Please what?" His voice was close to her ear.

"Please don't hurt me, Sir."

"Oh, I have no intention of harming one hair on this pretty little head." His heat disappeared.

She waited and listened but didn't hear anything. The chair she was sitting in began to rise, and she let out a cry.

"Easy." Cameron's voice was nearby. "I'm just getting you in position."

"For what?" Damn, she wished she could see. Where the hell were they? She tried to use her shoulder to nudge the blindfold away. A slap to her inside thigh had her jerking her head up.

"Leave the blindfold alone. I can't have you identifying me to the authorities."

"But they've already seen you." She let out a giggle.

"That was a friend. He'll never tell on me." The chair jerked to a stop.

Kristen just hoped the chair was well anchored. She didn't want to topple over.

Chapter Eighteen

Cameron grinned as he stood beside the chair. It was ingenious to have a movable platform under the chair. He stayed close as it rose to the height he wanted. Jack had shown it to him last week since it had just been installed. It had given Cameron ideas—ones that had included Kristen—hence today's little scene.

She was now about four feet off the ground and in perfect position. He looked her over. Her pussy was glistening with her excitement, her nipples hard, and her breathing erratic. Perfect.

Cameron made sure the platform was locked in place and went over to the small table. What to use on his captive? He picked up the nipple clamps with the chain and the wand. He'd never used a massage wand on her before and was curious to see her reaction. But first, the clamps.

"Such rosy nipples begging for attention...I think I'll give it to them." He began flicking her right nipple with his nail, watching it harden more. He played with her other nipple. When it grew hard, he opened the clamp and put it on.

"Ohhh." She breathed in and let it out slowly.

He did the second one before she finished her exhale.

"Damn." Her chin went up. She could tilt her head back a little before hitting the back of the chair.

Cameron tugged the chain between her breasts that connected the nipple clamps together.

"Shit," she cried.

He dropped the chain, letting it rest between her breasts, and she breathed in and out. He positioned himself in front of her. Luckily, the platform fit exactly to the dimension of the chair so he could maneuver without worrying.

Cameron slid between her spread legs and ran his fingers around her swollen labia. "So soft, so pretty and wet." He spread her wetness around and brushed her clit.

She wiggled and bucked, but she wasn't going anywhere. Using two fingers, he parted her pussy lips and smiled at her distended clit. Oh yes, she was more than ready.

He positioned the massage wand just below her clit and turned it on low.

A squeal escaped her lips, and her muscles tensed. He maneuvered the wand around her clit and her pussy lips, letting the vibrations do their job. Her pelvis began to twitch and shift from front to back ever so slightly.

Cameron glanced up at her face. Her mouth was open, her chest rising and falling with rapid breaths, the chain jiggling with her movements.

"So beautiful," he whispered and adjusted the wand, putting more pressure on her clit.

"Oh God," she cried, trying to push her hips up but was unable to from the way she was restrained in the chair.

"What do you want, my sweet?"

"Nothing from you." Her words were forced, and Cameron had to chuckle. She was still playing her role.

"Oh, really." He slid the wand up and down against her clit, knowing the vibrations were driving her closer and closer to orgasm.

"No, no, no." Her head swung from side to side.

"Oh, yes." He flipped the switch, putting the wand on high.

Her toes curled, and she let out a moan. "You bastard."

A flush filled her body, and her climax was on the cusp. It wouldn't take much to throw her over. He reached up, loosened the clamps on her nipples, and yanked the chain hard. The clamps came off her nipples.

Kristen screamed as her climax let loose, her body vibrating against the chair. He flipped the wand off and slid it away from her clit as she sagged in her bonds.

"So fucking beautiful." Cameron rose and captured her lips in a hard kiss.

He released her and put the wand and clamps back on the table. Then he lowered the platform. Once it was locked on the floor, he began undoing the restraints.

Her arms fell loosely to her sides. Cameron snatched the blanket from the table, and he pulled her to her feet. He wrapped the blanket around her and lifted her into his arms.

As he walked to the sofa, she laid her head on his shoulder and snuggled close. Cameron sat down, holding her. He ran his hands up and down her arm and back. "Okay?" he asked as satisfaction flowed through him. He'd given her a fantasy, and from her reactions, she'd enjoyed it.

"Mmm." She buried her face in his neck.

"Kristen, honey." He touched her cheek.

"Deliciously, thoroughly, and completely satisfied."

Cameron let out a laugh and tightened his arms around her, letting her rest. His cock was hard and wanting, but he could wait. He let his head fall back against the sofa.

"Cameron." A male voice penetrated his consciousness.

His eyes opened. Jack stood next to the sofa with two bottles of water.

"Hey, Jack." Cameron glanced down at Kristen, slumbering in his arms. After their late night last night and their early morning, he wasn't surprised she was asleep.

"I take it the scene went as you planned." Jack opened one bottle and handed it to him.

"Pretty much." Cameron raised the bottle to his lips and downed half of it. "What time is it?"

"Almost eleven."

He'd picked Kristen up at a little before eight; they'd arrived at the club about nine. After that, he'd lost track of time.

"Do you need me to get out of your hair?" Cameron asked.

"No, we're good. I'm not expecting anyone for a little bit." Jack gazed down at Kristen. "She's perfect for you."

"I know." And that didn't scare him as it might once have. Kristen had found his way into his heart and soul.

Kristen heard low male voices and tried to surface from her impromptu nap in Cameron's arms. A smile curved her lips as she remembered the intense orgasm

Cameron had given her. Hell, the whole scene had been one emotional roller coaster.

"Are you still thinking about going back to Scotland?" a male voice asked. *Jack.* They were in the club.

"Maybe."

Her breath caught in her throat. *What?* Cameron hadn't mentioned that he was planning on going back to Scotland. What did that mean for them? Their relationship? She opened her eyes.

Cameron gazed down at her, his face filled with passion. "How you doing?"

"Good." She started to sit up.

Cameron tightened his arm around her. "Just lay here for a few more minutes."

"Here," Jack said.

She looked up. Jack held an open bottle of water.

"Thanks." She slipped her arm out and took the bottle.

"No problem." He shifted on his feet as if he was uncomfortable. "Well, you've got about thirty minutes before I need to do inventory around the club."

"That's fine." Cameron's gaze briefly went to Jack as he left. He glanced back to her. "How are you feeling?"

"Good. That was one intense scene." She took another drink.

"Yes, it was. I apologize if Jack and I scared you in the beginning."

"Cameron." She lifted her hand and touched his cheek. "I might have been frightened, but inside, I knew you would protect me no matter what. Even though we talked about this and worked it all out, I just didn't realize it was part of the scene. My fantasy."

"At first, I thought you were just playing along. I'm embarrassed to say I didn't see the signs sooner."

"No need." Warmth filled her at his caring tone. "Once you reminded me about my safewords, everything fell into place. I just needed to pause to catch my breath."

"You are so beautiful." He dropped a kiss on her forehead, and shifted. He lifted her and placed her on the sofa. "Stay there and rest, I'm going to clean up. Then we'll go to my place.

Cameron jogged across the room and started the cleanup as her mind raced a mile a minute. How soon was Cameron going to leave? Why was he going back to Scotland? Wasn't she good enough for him?

When had she'd become so attached to him? It had happened gradually, and now she was in deep. She pushed down her feelings of doom. If he chose to leave... No she wouldn't think that way. They had something special together. She'd fight to keep him with her and pray she didn't get her heart broken, but she feared it was too late.

****

Kristen was too quiet. Cameron watched her push food around her plate over dinner at his parents' house.

After the scene, Jack had driven them back to Cameron's car and then they'd gone to his house. Not wanting to totally tire her out, they'd spent the afternoon curled up on the sofa, watching movies.

But they hadn't talked much. Even now over dinner as his family talked and discussed their day, Kristen was usually quiet.

"So, the Highland games next weekend..." his dad

started.

"Everything is in place," Cameron said. This was their year to make sure the vendors were in place, all the traditional games were available to those who wanted to play, and everything had flowed smoothly.

"I've checked in with each clan who wanted to participate in the games. They're ready," Alec said.

"The venue will be open to us at six Saturday morning, so vendors can get set up," Graham said.

"The drum and pipe corps are ready," Ian added.

"I'm working with Kristen, but I've checked with the food vendors as well. All is set up there," Skye said.

"See. Our kids have it well in hand." His mom patted his father's hand where it rested on the table. "So, Kristen, what surprises do you have in store for us this year?"

Kristen jumped, and she tensed up. He heard her let out a breath as her muscles relaxed.

"Now, if I told you that, it wouldn't be a surprise." Kristen's lips tilted up, but it wasn't the smile he was used to seeing from her.

His dad let out a laugh. "A woman who can keep a secret."

Better than anyone knew. Cameron searched her face, trying to figure out why she was so secretive, but she just kept smiling.

He pushed back his chair. "If you'll excuse us, Kristen and I have plans."

"Good thing you have a nice big—"

"Ian." His mother batted his arm.

"Bed, Mom. Bed."

"It was a great meal, Tira," Kristen said and glanced at his father. "Looking forward to the games,

Reid. I always love seeing all the men in kilts."

"My favorite part." Skye let out a laugh.

Cameron escorted her out of his parents' place. The drive back to his house was silent, and once they were back and sitting in his family room, he turned to her. "Out with it."

"What?" She folded her hands onto her lap, looking all Miss Prim and Proper.

"Kristen." He puffed out a breath. "Tell me what's wrong?"

"Nothing. I'm fine, Cameron, just a bit tired. Someone kind of wore me out today."

"It's more than tiredness." Damn, but this woman had his stomach in knots. "Did I cross the line today with the scene?" They had talked after the scene, but he was aware that intense scenes could create issues that surfaced hours or even days later.

She shook her head.

"Words, Kristen." He wanted to hear from her lips he hadn't screwed up.

"When Jack pulled us over, I got nervous. It wasn't until he pulled me out of the car and cuffed me that I got scared." She took a breath. "As I told you earlier, I'd totally forgotten we were in a scene once we left my apartment."

"Was it a good forget or a bad one?"

"A bit of both. I was scared, but you were there with me, and I knew you would protect me. It wasn't until you reminded me of my safewords that I remembered you promised to give me my fantasy."

"And did I?"

"More than you know." Her hand rose and her palm cradled his cheek. "Once I realized you were in total control, I relaxed. You and Jack had me going when you kept changing your voices."

"I was pretty sure you'd recognize his voice, so I wasn't taking any chances."

"I probably would have, but why did we go to the club?"

"Because you would have known my house, and at the club, we could use the chair."

"Ah yes, that diabolical chair."

Cameron laughed, and the tension seeped from his bones. She was talking to him, so that was good. And she wasn't upset. The Dom and man were both pleased. "You looked so very delicious, bound and open to whatever I wanted."

"I never realized the chair rose from the floor."

"Jack just installed the lift this week. We were the first test run."

"Oh my God, I'm glad it worked."

"Me, too." He slid his arm around her shoulders and cradled her to his side. "So…do you want to watch a movie, or just go cuddle in bed?"

"Actually, if you don't mind, I'd like to go home."

Cameron glanced down at her face. She seemed relaxed.

"I'm tired, Cameron." She brushed a kiss against his chin. "I sleep much better when I'm home. Plus, tomorrow I have to start figuring out everything I'm going to bake for the games."

"I guess I did wear you out today."

"Last night and today. But I enjoyed every second of it."

The sincerity etched in her face told him everything was all right. "Good, that was the plan.

Okay, let's get you home." He slapped her on the ass, and she jumped.

Thirty minutes and a few dozen kisses later, Cameron pulled away from the café. He'd wanted to stay, but Kristen had shooed him away, saying she'd never get any rest with him around. In a way, she was right.

Once back home, he flopped down on the sofa and flipped on a baseball game, but his mind wasn't on the game. It was on Kristen and his pending decision about Scotland.

He was losing his heart to her, and that should make his decision easier. But instead, it complicated it. Her business was here as was her life, and he wouldn't ask her to give that up. While he hadn't made any promises to return, he had agreed to give it serious consideration.

Chapter Nineteen

Early Saturday morning, Kristen turned onto the driveway that led to the parking lot for the vendors where the Highland Games were being held.

"A very good morning to you, Kristen," Ian said as she pulled the van to a halt. "Welcome to the Highland Games." He leaned against the open window of the small van she'd rented.

"Morning, Ian."

He reached into the small pouch he wore and pulled out a wristband. "Hold out your arm, please."

She held out her left wrist, and Ian fastened a red band on it. "What's this for?" They hadn't done this before.

"So you can freely access everything the games have to offer. Go ahead and follow the driveway. We've got your spot all marked out. Have fun." Ian stepped back.

Kristen followed Ian's directions—not that it was difficult. Cameron waved her into a parking spot. She turned the engine off and unlocked the doors.

"About time you got here." Cameron opened the door, undid her seat belt, and helped her out of the van. Then before she could even say a word, his lips covered hers.

She melted into his arms. He'd been such a good sport over the last week as she had experimented and baked. While it cut into their time together, she had made sure to spend as much free time with him as she could, and also included him while she was baking. She was excited about today and being with Cameron.

"Come on, big brother, quit groping your lady so we can get her set up and get some food." Alec's voice intruded.

Cameron broke the kiss. "Bug off."

Kristen laughed and placed her fingers against his lips. "He's right."

Cameron let out a big sigh. "All right, show us what needs to be done." He let his arms slip from around her, and instantly, she missed his warmth.

Last night, she'd finally decided to just enjoy their time together. She hadn't the courage to ask him if he was going back to Scotland, maybe because part of her didn't want to know. She wanted to deal with the here and now. That was her motto for today.

"Tents are in the back," Kristen said. "That needs to be put up first."

"Let's get this show on the road," Alec said, opening the back door.

Within a half-hour, her tent was set up along with all her tables, and now, the guys were carrying the food. Some would stay in the van where she had coolers and two small refrigerators. Specialized electrical cords had already been run to where she was set up.

The sun was rising. There were a few clouds in the sky, but all in all, it promised to be a nice day. Not too hot and not too cold. A good mix for late April in the Pacific Northwest.

"Coffee." She handed them both cups from the big carafe she'd brewed before leaving the café.

"Life saver." Alec sipped his brew and let out a satisfied groan.

"Oh good, the guys have done the hard work," Skye said as she strode up.

"Don't you look great?" Kristen admired Skye's kilt that flowed right around her knees. It was a mixture of deep maroon, yellow, green, and a blue-green—the clan McMillan colors. Kristen was familiar with them.

"Thanks." Skye gave a little curtsy.

"Isn't that skirt a little short?" Alec asked.

"It's fine." Skye frowned at her brother. "You two better go get dressed."

"True." Cameron snagged Kristen around the waist. "Be back shortly. Did you bring any blueberry scones?"

"For you, I did." She grinned. "I'll keep them warm." She had them in insulated bags with warming gel packs.

"A woman after my heart." He dropped a soft kiss against her lips before sauntering off with his brother.

His words lingered in her mind. They hadn't spoken of more than just dating, and with the possibility of him going back to Scotland, she wondered if she really had his heart. Maybe food-wise.

She glanced around at the empty tables. "Let's get things set up," she said to Skye.

"Things look delicious," Reid McMillan said as he and his wife strode up to her tent an hour later.

Kristen smiled. They looked so adorable dressed in the McMillan tartan and holding hands. Had her parents ever held hands?

"I'm so glad you're set up already," Reid said, his black hair gleaming in the light. "Bear claw and coffee, please."

"Reid." Tira let out a sigh and shook her head, the hair piled up on top waggling.

"Hush, woman, it's just one day."

Kristen's gaze went from Tira to Reid and back.

"His sugar has been a little high," Tira said.

"A little. I'm fine."

"Men," Tira huffed but nodded.

Kristen got him his food and drink. "Tira?"

"Strawberry scone and juice, please."

She quickly got Tira's order while Skye helped another couple who had walked up.

"How much?" Reid asked.

"Put your money away." Kristen shook her head. "On the house."

Tira nodded her thanks. "Make sure Cameron takes you around so you can check out all the vendors. Reid and I have to make sure everything is set up for the dance competition." With a wave, the couple set off.

Kristen moved to help another couple then turned to ask Skye a question and stopped dead.

Cameron strode toward her in a long sleeved white shirt with a vest made of tartan and... Her brain short circuited. Yes, she'd seen him in a kilt before, but today...the maroon, yellow, green, and green-blue colors brought out the blueness of his eyes, and he looked utterly lickable.

"Hello again, lass," he said, using a Scottish accent.

"My lord." She gave him a little curtsy. "And may I say your knees look quite handsome today."

Cameron burst out laughing. "They're behaving just for you." He motioned her to come out of the tent.

She grinned and stepped out.

He said, "Turn around, back to me."

"Okay." She turned, wondering what he was up to.

"Raise your arms slightly and close your eyes, please."

His "please" had her doing as he asked. His body heat singed her back when he leaned close. His hand spread between her breasts as he held something in place, then it was draped around her shoulder, wrapped around to her back, and tugged until tight.

"You can lower your arms and open your eyes."

Kristen did and looked down. Tears sprang to her eyes. Cameron had taken some of the McMillan tartan and fashioned a sash for her to wear. It was held together with a pin in the shape of a sword.

"Oh my goodness." She turned to him. "Thank you." She flung her arms around his neck and kissed him.

"My special lady should be decked out in my colors with my family crest." He hugged her close. "Later, I want to see you draped in nothing but my family tartan."

Kristen ducked her head and heat invaded her cheeks. But anticipation shot through her body, causing her nipples to harden.

"But for now, I have work to do. I'll be back later to take you around and to show you something special." He released her and ambled away.

Kristen went back into her tent, feeling like a princess, and Skye smiled at her.

"That looks good on you," Skye said.

"Thanks." Kristen couldn't keep the grin off her face. He'd given her the family tartan...that had to mean something, right? Maybe, just maybe, it meant he would stay.

****

"Go." Skye said hours later as she made a shooing motion with her hands. "I've got this covered."

Kristen looked from Skye to Cameron and back to the tent's counter with waiting customers. It was early afternoon, but they had a steady stream of business, buying coffee, cakes, and cookies. She didn't want to leave Skye alone. "We've been really busy."

"I'm fine." Skye huffed out a breath. "Get her out of here Cameron before she thinks up an excuse. She's been wanting to explore all morning."

"Come on." Cameron slipped his arm around her waist and guided her away from her food tent. "So what's first on the agenda?"

"Meat pies." Skye was right; she had been wanting to get out and see everything and taste the food.

"As my lady wishes."

"So many vendors," Kristen said after they had gotten their meat pies, motioning with her hand to the rows of tents as she and Cameron walked toward a picnic table with a tray of food.

"Yep. I'll take you shopping in a bit." Cameron set their tray onto the table.

"I can't believe you got all this." She gestured to the overflowing tray.

"You said you were hungry." He waited until she sat down before taking a seat next to her.

"Hungry, yes. But how much do you think I eat?"

Cameron laughed. "Just means more for me." He picked up the knife and fork, cutting a piece of the meat pie and holding it out to her.

"I can feed myself." She looked at the tray. Cameron had made sure to only grab one set of utensils and one plate. This reminded her of the night at the restaurant. She hadn't minded then, and now…she glanced around. People weren't paying attention to them at all.

"Yes, but it will be my pleasure to take care of my lady." He put the morsel up to her mouth. Her lips parted, and he slipped it in.

"That is delicious," she said after swallowing the savory beef.

"Good. Just think…tonight while you're lying in bed, wearing nothing but my tartan, I can feed you more delicious treats."

"Cameron." She glanced around, but no one was close enough to hear him.

"Just letting you know that tonight, you're mine."

Anticipation flowed through her blood. There was nothing she wanted more than to be his.

Chapter Twenty

An hour later, Cameron guided Kristen past the bags and pipes players, dancers, and the Highland Game's check-in stations set up in the shelter of the trees. His nerves tingled with anticipation.

"Where are we going?"

"You'll see," Cameron said, keeping their destination a secret. He wanted to surprise her. How would she react to the Kinky Highland Games? It had taken some convincing, but he was allowed to use one of the back buildings to set up an area where adults could be educated on kink if they wanted.

He led her past the wooden stalls toward the big, wooden building in the back that used to be a dance barn in the old days. There were a few people wandering this way, and he was glad. Since he'd championed for this, he hoped people would take advantage in this setting.

He escorted her up the ancient plank steps to the oak door guarded by his brother, Graham.

Graham said, "I wondered when you'd bring her back here."

"What is in here?" Kristen asked.

Cameron grinned down at her as Graham pushed open the door. "Welcome to the Kinky Highland Games."

Cameron guided Kristen into the old dance barn,

checking to make sure everything was going well. Thanks to Jack, he'd been able to convince the Highland Games committee to allow him to run the Kinky Highland Games. He was pleased to see a lot of people inside the barn, watching the demonstrations and talking with Doms and subs.

After his six months in Scotland in an educational swap, he'd come home with renewed energy and had been convinced that education was the key to having people understand the alternative lifestyle. Having such education at the Highland Games was a chance to reach a larger group of people since there were people her from neighboring cities.

The two main stages were draped in various tartans and set up for demonstrations or lectures. The adult "goodies" vendors were set up along the walls as well. There were floggers, adult toys, whips, DVDs, books, and there was a separate educational table. Several couples milled around, looking at items and talking with those educating and the vendors.

There were chairs and tables spread around the old dance floor were filled. Those were set up so people could sit and talk, plus several of the Doms and subs from the club were available to answer questions and do whatever else was needed.

They'd opened their doors at eleven, and now at almost one, attendance was looking good. Graham was manning the entrance to make sure no one without a red wristband entered. And everyone was dressed in traditional kilts, much to the dismay of some of the Doms who balked at wearing what they considered a skirt. But the Doms wore them out of respect for the Highland Games.

"Holy crap, how did you manage this?" Kristen exclaimed.

"Jack helped. Well, actually, a lot of the Doms from Decadence did." He guided her over to the side, out of the walkway.

"This is... I don't know what to say."

"I wanted the community to have more education, and this seemed the best way."

Kristen looked around. "How do you stop kids from coming in here?"

"By always having someone at the door...and this." He flicked her red wristband.

She smiled. "I wondered what that was for."

"Yes, everyone is given a flyer when they arrive about the Kinky Highland Games. If they're interested, they sign a waiver and are given a red wristband."

"I didn't sign a waiver. Ian just put this on my wrist."

"That's because they all know you're with me." He grinned. "Want to look around?"

"Hell, yes!"

Cameron couldn't help but laugh at the excitement in her voice. "Let's go."

Kristen grinned at him when he pulled her to a stop at one of the demo stations. Paul and Will were set up there, giving massages and discussing techniques. The woman they had on the massage table let out little moans of pleasure as they massaged her back.

Cameron turned his head to see the mayor and his wife. He nodded at the mayor, who nodded back. Kristen stiffened in his hold, and he snapped his attention back to her.

"What's wrong?" he whispered.

She shook her head, but he wasn't going to let her get away with that. He guided her away from the massage area to a space that was empty at the moment. He turned her to face him. "Tell me."

Kristen let out a sigh. "The mayor saw us."

"So?" What was going through that pretty head of hers?

"Cameron, I have a business. I didn't think this through, people seeing me here, knowing I'm interested…" She waved her hands in the air.

"And they're here for the same reason." He cupped her cheek. "Sweetheart, if they judge you because they saw you here, then they are the hypocrite. There is nothing wrong with being curious or being in the lifestyle."

"I know here." She placed her hand on her heart. "You are right. But here…" She touched her temple. "It's a little harder to reconcile."

"Do you want to leave?" He did understand her point, and he would defer to her on this if she wanted to leave.

"Please." She glanced at her watch. "I've been gone from my tent for over an hour, I really need to get back and help Skye."

"Then we'll go," Cameron reluctantly agreed. He was disappointed, but he did understand. She was still nervous about people knowing she was into kink.

Hand in hand, he escorted her back to her tent. "I'll see you later." He brushed a quick kiss over her lips before sauntering away.

Kristen stood in front of the tent, staring at Cameron, admiring the way his ass looked in his kilt before turning to see Skye smiling at her.

"Did you have fun?" Skye asked.

Kristen glanced down to see the red wristband on Skye's wrist. "You knew?"

Skye nodded.

"Does everyone know?" She shook her head. What did it matter anymore? She was sure people had already seen her inside the Kinky Highland Games. She was her own woman. There was no reason for people to look down on her. She was an adult, capable of making her own decisions. But she hoped people didn't judge her for her decision.

"Probably not, only those who are into kink or curious." Skye touched her arm. "There's no shame in it."

"No there isn't." And there wasn't. Now she wished she hadn't said anything to Cameron about being uncomfortable. They could have spent more time together. Kristen glanced around. "Are your parents aware?"

"That all us kids are involved? Yep." Skye grinned. "They shake their heads at us, but then Mom says, 'To each their own.' And Dad says, 'Go get 'em.' "

Kristen laughed. "Why don't you take some time for yourself now? I'll handle everything here."

"I'll be back to help you close down." Skye danced off, and Kristen couldn't help but laugh.

****

Kristen hid a yawn behind her hand. The games had closed at five, and because she was virtually sold out of everything, there wasn't much to pack up. The tables and tent were left up for the next day.

"Meet you at your place," Cameron said as she started the engine on the van.

"Okay." She pulled away after Cameron stepped back. The day had been fun, and she really wanted to explore more of the Kinky Highland Games tomorrow. Once back at the café, Kristen quickly unloaded the empty trays and turned on the ovens.

Tim had left her a note that everything had gone well today, that he'd put all the money in the safe, and that he'd be in at six thirty Monday morning. Kristen let out a sigh. She had to bake enough stuff for tomorrow, and then tomorrow deal with Monday. Some days, it really did seem never-ending.

A knock sounded at the back door.

"Who is it," she asked as she padded over to it, very aware she was alone.

"Cameron."

She unlocked the door and pulled it open.

"Thank you," he said, dropping a kiss on her forehead.

"For what?"

"For asking who it was." He pushed past her, and Skye and his brothers followed.

Her mouth dropped open. "What are all of you doing here?"

"We're going to help you," Skye said, going over to the rack and grabbing a handful of aprons.

"What?" Kristen shook her head as tears blurred her vision.

"Help. All of us." Cameron chucked her under the chin. "I know you have a lot to get done, so it will be easier if we help."

This time, the tears did spill over.

"Baby." Cameron drew her into his arms.

"I'm okay." She sniffled. "Thank you," she

whispered. Then with a big inhale, she pushed away from Cameron. "Thank you, all."

"Just show us what to do, and we promise not to eat all the profits," Ian said.

By ten that night, all her goods were baked or ready to be baked first thing in the morning. Her kitchen was clean, and Cameron was seeing his brothers and sister off.

Kristen's heart was bursting from amazement.

She'd never had people so unselfishly take time away from their lives to help her out. A very unique experience for her. The shutting of the back door and click of the lock had her turning to see Cameron. Tears clouded her eyes.

"Sweetheart, what is it?" His long strides carried him to her, and he took her by the shoulders.

"You, Skye, and your brothers are so wonderful," she whispered.

"And that is making you cry?" He frowned, confusion written on his face.

"Yes." She gave a laugh. "I've never had anyone who cared so much aside from my grandmother."

"Oh, Kristen." Cameron brushed a tear away with his thumb. "I do care, and I didn't want you coming back here and spending all night baking. Skye had already volunteered, and when my brothers heard, nothing could keep them away."

"It was perfect." She slipped her arms around his waist and hugged him.

"What will be perfect is you and I taking a quick shower and then curling up in bed together."

"You're staying?"

"Yep. I'll help you load tomorrow. Besides, I'll

sleep better, knowing you're resting in my arms."

"Let's go." She entwined her fingers with his and pulled him toward the stairs to her apartment. The day just kept getting better and better. Tomorrow would take care of itself.

****

The next afternoon, Cameron breathed a sigh of relief. The games would officially close in an hour. The Kinky Highland Games were mostly packed up. Tomorrow after his university classes were over, he'd come help Jack and the others tear down the stages and move the equipment back to Decadence. While he loved the games, they had also tired him out. Not to mention a certain little café owner.

He thought back to last night. They'd made more cookies than he could imagine they'd need. He, along with his brothers, had learned about using cookie cutters and how to make sure the dough was placed just right on the trays and after they'd finished baking. Kristen and Skye had decorated and drizzled chocolate while the boys baked. A grin spread over his lips. He'd loved how Kristen's body had cradled against his as they slept. And then he remembered him swearing when the alarm went off at six. But now, the late night with little sleep was catching up with him.

A short while after checking the games venue to make certain all was going well, he returned to Kristen's tent, surprised to see a line of people. What was going on?

"Oh thank God, reinforcements," Skye said when she spotted him. "Get back here."

"What's going on?" he asked.

"Here." Skye shoved a pad and paper in his hand.

"Start there." She pointed to the sixth woman in line. "Write down their name, what they want, and how many. Kristen and I will fill. They can't have more than two dozen."

He was about to ask "two dozen what" when a woman said, "My name is Jessie. I want six Scotties, six kilts, and a dozen shortbread."

Cameron nodded, wrote it down, ripped the piece of paper off, and handed it to Skye. And off they went. He took orders while Kristen filled box after box with cookies and Skye took the money.

"That's it, we're out." Kristen called with still about a dozen people in line. "I'm sorry. Add your phone number to your order, and I'll make them up special this week."

"And I'll deliver to anyone local," Cameron said.

The people remaining cheered, gave Cameron their orders, and left.

Kristen sank down onto the grass. "Well, I would say the cookies were a success."

"No kidding." Skye joined her.

"Hey, Cameron, where are your sister and Kristen?" his father asked, walking up to him.

Cameron gestured to them leaning against each other on the ground.

"That busy?" His father shook his head.

"I can't believe it." Skye pushed her hair away from her face. "I think we made more in the last two hours than we made all of yesterday."

"I can't move," Kristen said.

"No worries," Reid said. "Boys, let's get a move on. Tear it down, and get it into the van."

"But…" Kristen started to move.

"Stay there," Cameron ordered.

"Yes, Sir." Kristen grinned, and Skye giggled.

****

A ringing woke Kristen. She rolled over...into a warm body. She frowned. Warm body?

Her lashes rose. Cameron was in bed with her. Well, there was nothing too unusual about that, except the last thing she remembered was parking the van outside the café.

"Would you silence that damn ringing?" Cameron asked, his voice husky with sleep.

She reached behind her and smacked her alarm clock.

"What time is it?"

"Four thirty." She gazed down at him. "How did I get to bed?"

"I carried you." His arms tightened around her waist. "You were all but asleep behind the wheel of the van. My brothers helped me unload then I carried you up here and put you to bed."

"I was out of it, wasn't I?"

"You had a pretty busy day."

"Yep." She tilted her head and kissed his cheek. "You are a very sweet man."

"Hey don't let that get out. I'm supposed to be the mean professor."

Kristen laughed as she slipped from his hold and walked toward the bathroom. "I guess I'll just have to take a shower alone if you're so mean."

With a growl, Cameron leaped out of bed and scooped her up into his arms. "No teasing, wench."

Chapter Twenty-One

The next week passed quickly. Kristen stayed busy baking and Cameron with his classes. She hadn't brought up the possibility of him leaving for Scotland, and he hadn't offered.

One Friday right after the lunch crowd left, the bell rang on the café door, and Kristen looked up to see Mrs. Johnson.

"I wonder what kind of gossip she's spreading today," Skye whispered from Kristen's side.

Kristen grinned. "Hello, Mrs. Johnson, what can I get for you today?"

"A moment of your time, dear Kristen." Mrs. Johnson patted her gray hair secured in a bun.

Kristen frowned but nodded. "Be right back," she said to Skye before joining Mrs. Johnson at one of the tables.

"Is there a problem?" Kristen sat down across from her.

"There could be, dear." Mrs. Johnson's hand fluttered to the table. "I understand you're seeing the oldest McMillan boy."

"Cameron, yes." Kristen tilted her head, wondering where this was going.

"Well, dear, I would rethink that."

"Excuse me?" This woman did not just tell her to stop seeing Cameron.

"I know you've only been in our community for a short time, and many admire Cameron for his teaching position, but his *other* activities concern people."

Kristen frowned, and her stomach tightened in a knot of fear. "Other activities?"

"You know about his involvement with that...sex club?" Mrs. Johnson whispered, looking around to see if anyone was listening.

"Mrs. Johnson—"

"You did know about it, didn't you, dear?" Her face lined with concern.

"Yes, I did." Kristen took a deep breath. "What Cameron does is his business."

"But, my dear, it can affect your business."

"What?" Her spine stiffened. "Are you implying the people of Grant would boycott my café because I'm seeing Cameron?"

"It's possible, dear. I just want you to be prepared. I certainly couldn't, in good conscience, continue to support a business where the owner is into kink." Mrs. Johnson stood up and marched out of the café.

Kristen was stunned. She'd finally made headway with her old fears of what people thought of her, of living up to other's expectations, and now this. A tremor shook her body. Fears of losing everything reared its ugly head. But she was stronger now and not so willing to roll over. No, she wouldn't give into this. She stood up and went behind the counter.

"All okay?" Skye asked.

"Fine. I'll be in the kitchen."

"Okay, Mary Lewis just called. She wants to know if she can get six dozen cookies in two hours," Skye called out from the café.

"Sure. Ask her what kind." Kristen shook her head to dispel Mrs. Johnson's words. The café was doing fine.

She got to work on the cookies as soon as Skye had told her what Mary wanted. The cookies were all ready and boxed up when Mary Lewis walked through the door in her daily hat and flowered dress.

"Hi Mary, I've got everything ready for you," Kristen said. She'd sent Skye on a break and was manning the counter.

"Thanks, Kristen."

Kristen sat the boxes on the counter. "Thirty dollars even." She took the money and gave Mary her change. "Thank you for your business."

Instead of picking up the boxes, Mary hesitated. "Kristen, I don't know if you know, but Mrs. Johnson has been saying some not so nice things lately."

She sighed. "She was in here this morning."

"She's spouting off about you and Cameron being an item and his involvement at Decadence."

Kristen's stomach clenched. "I don't know what to say." She refused to defend herself, because there was nothing to defend against.

"You don't need to say anything. What you and Cameron do is your business; you're both adults. I just thought you should know." Mary picked up her boxes and left.

Kristen slumped against the counter. Well, that just sucked. What was she going to do?

"Hey," Skye said, and Kristen jumped. "Sorry, didn't mean to scare you. Would you mind if I left early?"

"No, go ahead." Kristen looked at the clock. It was

almost four, and the place was empty. "Oh the heck with it. Let's just close up early today."

She needed some down time. She'd been so busy with the café, her relationship with Cameron, and the Highland games, she could use a night off.

Skye looked startled but began helping Kristen close up. Within thirty minutes, they had the place cleaned up, everything put away, and the money in the safe.

"I'll see you tomorrow." Skye waved as she went out the back door. Kristen locked the door behind her.

She really should do some baking, but between Mrs. Johnson's veiled threat and Cameron's possible departure, her heart wasn't in it. She trudged up the steps to her apartment, flopped down on the sofa, and turned on the TV. A few hours vegging in front of the television would make her feel better. It had to.

****

A week later, Kristen stood at the counter and sighed. She was a coward. She hadn't talked to Cameron yet about what Mrs. Johnson had said. Heck, she hadn't mentioned it to anybody. Instead, she had let it stew in her brain. Cameron had been prepping for finals, but that didn't mean she couldn't talk to him. This was all on her. Now, finals at the college were in full swing, and while they'd had a morning rush, now, it was pretty quiet.

It would be this way until about two until when the early finals were done and the hordes would descend around four when the rest of them were done.

While Kristen wanted to talk to someone about what Mrs. Johnson had said, she didn't want to give voice to her own fears. She didn't want to face up to them being true. So instead of talking with Skye, she checked the supplies and let Skye handle anyone who came in.

The bell rang, and Kristen's lips turned up. She loved the sound of that bell. She waited, but didn't hear anything. Curious, she made her way out of the kitchen.

Cameron stood with Skye, quietly talking. His head lifted, and Kristen's breath caught in her throat. His blue eyes were blazing, his face stiff and tight.

Skye turned around. "Ummm, yeah take Kristen out. I can handle the café."

"Thanks, sis." Cameron marched over to her and cupped her elbow. "We need to talk."

Kristen didn't protest. She waited until they were in Cameron's SUV before she asked, "What's going on? Don't you have finals?"

"An intervention."

"What?" She fastened her seat belt and Cameron pulled out of the driveway.

"Kristen, some guy is in town, asking a lot of questions about you and the café."

Her mouth dropped open. "Some guy? How long has he been in town, asking questions?" She racked her brain, trying to figure out why someone would be asking about her. She could only think of one reason— her parents.

"A week. I just heard about it today." His fingers tightened on the steering wheel. "One of my students mentioned to me today that the guy had been hanging around outside the café, asking questions about you."

Kristen swore under her breath. This was so not good.

"Do you know who the guy is?"

She thought back over the last week, all the customers in her café, all the usual people and... She shook her head but then remembered a guy hanging out in front of the café. Skye had made a comment that she'd seen him the last few days. "Medium-build guy with light brown hair and glasses?"

"You know him?"

"No, but he was in the café last week."

"And you didn't think to tell me that." He took one hand off the wheel to rake through his hair.

"Why would I?" She tangled her fingers together. "I just figured he was driving through. He never approached me." She didn't know what to think. "Where are we going?"

"To meet this guy."

"What?" She twisted in her seat as much as the seat belt would allow her. "Are you crazy?"

"No. I want to get to the bottom of this. So when this guy came to the college today, I arranged for us to meet."

"Cameron, this isn't a good idea."

"No?" He turned toward Decadence. "What are you hiding?"

"Nothing." Her family couldn't have found her, could they? She'd changed her name to avoid being found.

Cameron pulled into the parking lot next to Decadence. "Why are we here?" she asked.

"I called Jack, and he's allowing me to use his office space next to the club to talk to this guy." Cameron turned off the vehicle and climbed out.

Kristen let out a sigh as she undid her seat belt and opened the door, but Cameron was there. When she slid out, he stood in front of her, his hand cupping her chin, raising her face up.

"Whatever it is, Kristen, we will face it together." He lowered his forehead to hers. "I will protect you, help you. I love you."

He loved her? Her breath caught in her throat. "I…" She couldn't get any words out. Her heart ached to tell him she loved him, too.

"Shhh." He cupped her cheek. "Later, we will discuss this, but for right now, I'm in your corner." He stepped back, slipped his arm around her waist, and guided her inside the building.

Cameron hadn't meant to blurt out that he loved her like that, but now that he had, he was glad.

First, Mrs. Johnson and her crap had upset him. When Mrs. Johnson had approached his mother and had started in on how Tira raised her son, he'd gone insane. His mother, bless her heart, had told Mrs. Johnson to take her judgmental words and put them where the sun doesn't shine, because her children were raised to be open and loving to all lifestyles.

He'd waited for Kristen to tell him about Mrs. Johnson, but she hadn't. He had to wonder why she still couldn't confide in him.

Now, this stranger was asking questions. Kristen was holding back by not telling him everything, and they would damn well get to the bottom of her reasons for shutting him out. Very soon.

He guided her into the room where his family was seated

"Cameron?" She stopped in her tracks.

"Together we stand," he whispered, guiding her farther into the room. Then two men at the end of the table stood, both in suits. But the one was the brown hair was the guy who'd been asking questions. The gray haired guy…Cameron had no idea who he was.

Kristen let out a gasp. "Mr. Reynolds?" Kristen's voice was shaky.

"You're a difficult person to track down, Kristen."

Kristen stiffened. "Maybe because I didn't want to be found."

"You've made that clear." There was no mistaking the derision in his voice.

Cameron took a step forward.

"No, Cameron." She tightened her hold on his hand. "Mr. Reynolds is my parents' high-priced lawyer. I don't know who the other gentleman is, but he is the one who was in the café last week."

"Steven Williams, private investigator," the man with the brown hair said.

"I've come to take you home," Reynolds said.

Chapter Twenty-Two

"Like hell." Kristen tore herself from Cameron's hold as she faced the group in Jack's office. "You can go back and tell them I'm never coming back. Ever."

It was time she stopped running and stood up to her family. Over the past few months, Cameron had shown her she was a woman with inner strength, one who wasn't going to hide anymore. Seeing Cameron and his family in the room helped strengthened her resolve. Their support, without even knowing why, not only warmed her heart but let her know she had a place. It was here in Grant with them.

"Don't be difficult, Kristen," Reynolds started.

"She doesn't need to be difficult. I can do that for her." Alec stepped forward. "Alec McMillan, legal counsel for Ms. Caldwell."

Kristen opened her mouth, and Cameron shook his head.

She closed it as Alec crossed the room to her and Cameron. "Kristen, you don't have to talk to him or anyone else."

"Thanks, Alec." Her lips turned up as happiness filled her soul.

"Since Caldwell isn't her real name, it hardly matters," Reynolds said.

"Shows how much you don't know." It was time to stand on her own two feet, but the knowledge Cameron would be there if she needed him was all the impetus she needed. "I legally changed my name to Caldwell."

Alec snickered. "Sounds like your PI didn't do such a good job."

"I want to talk to Kristen alone," Reynolds said.

"Not happening," Cameron said.

"And there is no reason for them to leave." Kristen placed her hands on her hips.

"Do you really want to air your dirty laundry in front of them?" Reynolds asked.

"That sounded like a threat." Alec took a step forward.

"My dirty laundry?" Kristen laughed. "Please. I can only guess as to why my so-called parents are so gung-ho to find me all the sudden. Did the press dig up something new, and they want me to be the scapegoat?"

Reynolds' face turned red, and Kristen let out a bitter laugh. "That's it, isn't it?" She threw her hands in the air. "Cameron knows my parents saw fit that anytime I made a mistake to make sure my misgivings got into the press so they could blame me for all their woes."

"They didn't support you?" Cameron's mom asked.

"No." She turned to face the McMillans. "But four years ago after my grandmother died, I'd had enough. I wanted to get away from my family." She wrapped her arms around her waist. "I had taken care of my grandmother since my parents couldn't be bothered. I wouldn't let her be put into a home. But she left me an inheritance. I moved to Grant, changed my name, and opened the café."

"You left your parents heartbroken," Reynolds

said.

"Oh, bull," she muttered. "My parents only cared for the Worthington name. They didn't care about me or what I wanted from life. They wanted the perfect, robot daughter. I couldn't step out of line. I had to make everyone happy but myself. And God forbid if I did something that caused people to think poorly of the Worthington name."

"It doesn't matter. You need to come back." Reynolds took a step forward.

"Whose army is going to do that?" Ian asked, as the entire family closed ranks around her. Protecting her. Her heart filled with so much love for her adopted family.

Reynolds gave them a sly grin before going to the door. He pushed it open, and in walked her parents. Her mother patted her perfectly coiffed, dyed-blonde hair. And her father cupped her mother's arm as she tried to walk on impossible high heels. Kristen glanced at her father. His hair was more white than brown, and he had lines of tiredness around his eyes.

"No," she whispered, allowing herself to sag against Cameron. They couldn't force her to go back, could they? She was a grown woman. Still, fear filled her veins.

"No one is going to make you do anything you don't want," Cameron whispered in her ear as if he read her mind.

"I know who you are," Tira said to her parents before turning to look at Kristen.

Kristen held her breath. Was Tira going to denounce her? Tell her she had to go back to her parents? Was the entire McMillan family going to turn against her?

"Thank goodness, Kristen doesn't take after either of you." Tira wrinkled her nose as if she smelled something really bad.

"Who are these people?" Kristen's mother asked in a tone that set her nerves on edge.

"We're her family." Reid stepped forward. "That's all you need to know."

"Excuse me—" Her father stepped forward. "—but I'm her Gordon, her father."

Kristen straightened, and Cameron tightened his hold on her waist. She appreciated his support, but it was time for her to take control of her life. She tilted her head and rose on her toes, brushing a kiss against his rigid jaw.

"It's okay," she whispered. She stiffened her spine and stepped away from Cameron's hold. Keeping her head up, she pushed between Ian and Alec. "You might be my biological father, but these people here are my true family."

"Stop this nonsense," Gordon ordered. "These people"—he waved his hand—"have obviously brainwashed you. You're coming home now."

"I'm not." Kristen was amazed at how strong her voice was. She wanted to run. She wanted to let Cameron and his family handle this. But she wouldn't. Time to put her family to rest.

"Don't talk back to me."

Kristen flinched at his harsh tone, but she wasn't going to back down. Hands settled on her shoulders. Cameron's hands. He always supported her, no matter what.

"First of all," Kristen started, "I'm thirty-two, not

two. Second of all, I'm a grown woman, and I will make my own decisions."

"Your decision is to come home," her father said as if he believed he had the right to order her around.

Kristen rolled her eyes. "I am home."

"But, darling girl," her mother started.

Oh Lord, she hated being called "darling girl," especially in her mother's whiny voice.

"You can't possibly want to live…well, here," her mother said.

The disdain in her voice made Kristen's gut clench. Her mother was such a snob.

"If you mean here in Grant, then yes." Kristen looked her mother in the eye. "I have a nice place to live, a thriving business, and people who care about me. Me, as a person, not as something to be brought out only when I'm useful."

"You're living above your café," her mother whined.

"Yes, and I love every minute of it."

"Enough." Her father took a step forward.

Kristen held her ground, not only holding Cameron back but his brothers as well.

"You will come home now, or I will tell the world about Cameron McMillan and his dirty ways."

"Excuse me?" Cameron's voice was clear and strong, but his body vibrated with anger.

"I will go to the college board and explain to them how you defiled my daughter, forced her to go to that dirty club, and how you beat her."

Kristen's face grew warm, but she reminded herself there was nothing wrong with what she and Cameron had done. They were consenting adults.

Cameron was shifting behind her, his muscles tensing up. She wanted to defuse this as quickly as possible but was unsure how.

"Go right ahead," Reid said.

Kristen's head turned to stare at Cameron's dad. Then Tira stepped forward, along with Alec, Graham and Ian.

"As you can see, it doesn't matter what you say, Cameron and Kristen have our support and our love."

Gordon snorted and trained his nasty glare on her. "What about your café? How will you feel when you have to close it because you have no customers?"

She winced. Damn. Her father knew right where it hurt. But there was more at stake here than her business. Cameron's career could be at risk.

"Drag me through the mud all you want, but Cameron and his family have done nothing wrong or illegal."

"They won't be dragging you anywhere." Cameron stepped in front of her. "Go ahead and talk to the university board. I think you might find they are already aware of my involvement at Decadence."

"You defiled our daughter," her mother cried out.

"He defiled nothing," Kristen shouted from behind Cameron as she forced her way between him and Alec again. Damn dominant males. "I've been my own woman for years now. What we did was consensual."

"It changes nothing," her father said.

"Oh, I say it changes everything," a new voice said.

Jack and the sheriff stood in the doorway. This just kept getting better and better. Soon, they'd have the whole town involved.

Her father glanced over his shoulder. "Who the hell are you?"

"Jack Christenson. I run Decadence."

"And I'm Sheriff Brooks." The sheriff moved into the room. "I've received several complaints about strangers in town, making threatening innuendos about the people in my town."

"You did?" Kristen didn't know why she was surprised. Her father could be a real ass at times.

"These people seemed to think this family is all smiles and sunshine, but they're not. They took my daughter away." Her father hands waved in the air as he spoke.

"You threw me away." It was as if her father's words broke the dam. "You didn't want a daughter, you wanted a showpiece, and when I wouldn't conform, you found ways to belittle me and try to force me to be what you wanted. Well I have news for you; I'm me, and I'll never be what you want." She was out of breath when she finished, but the weight she'd been carrying around disappeared. No more running, no more hiding. She'd found her true home and nothing, no one, was going to take it away from her.

"We only wanted what was best for you," her father said.

"You wanted what was best for you and your so-called friends. Enough of this. You aren't wanted here." Kristen was proud at how steady her voice was.

"Hear, hear," Jack said.

"We'll ruin everyone in this town!" her father raged.

"Just try." Jack's shoulders drew back, and Kristen watched the Dom come out. "I have a team of lawyers on speed dial, plus the press. Shall I prove to you who has the bigger balls?"

"Now there's an image I could live without," Tira muttered.

Kristen burst out laughing. She couldn't help it. Soon, almost everyone was laughing.

Her father's face grew red. "Let's go. I'll inform the media." He spun on his heel.

Her mother gave her a haughty look and followed before Reynolds sidled around the tight knit group to follow her parents.

Only the PI remained. "I don't have a hand in this game. They hired me to find her, and that was it. If you need me, I'm more than willing to talk." He pulled out his card and handed it to the sheriff before moving to the door. "Nice town you got here."

Kristen tilted her head, and it was then she heard voices. Loud of voices. She strode over to the door and her jaw dropped open. The local news agency was outside.

"We're outside the Christenson building, and it's as if the entire town of Grant is here. The reason for this gathering is because these people"—the female reporter waved her hands in the direction of her parents and lawyer—"are trying to force one of our own, Kristen Caldwell, beloved owner of the Cozy Corners Café, to go with them. From what this reporter has found out, these people are the well-known Worthington family from California."

Kristen let out a breath. Well, the cat was out of the bag. Not that she cared anymore. No matter what happened, she had a place in this town.

"The Worthingtons used to be worth billions, but in

the last five years, they've squandered away their fortune. From other reports, because Kristen left, they allegedly could no longer sell their stories about their poor, distraught daughter to the tabloids."

Her body sagged, and Cameron's arms went around her waist, holding her against him as he cursed. Her parents had sold her out to the tabloids? Not her boyfriends like she thought?

"In our investigative research, we found out that they need their daughter to shore up their finances. But as they have seen, there is a lot of support in Grant for Ms. Caldwell. The Cozy Corner café owner won't be going anywhere she doesn't want to. Not if this town has anything to say about it."

"Let's get out of here," Alec muttered.

"Good idea."

The group slipped away.

****

Hours later after Kristen had explained everything to her new family, she and Cameron were finally alone at his place.

Snuggled up on the sofa, TV playing quietly in the background, Kristen hated to ruin the peace they found, but there was still one thing they needed to settle.

"Are you planning to go back to Scotland?" she blurted out.

Cameron stiffened. "Why do you think that?"

She maneuvered herself as best as she could since she was lying on him until she could see his face. "I heard you and Jack talking after the scene we had together."

"That was over a month ago."

She nodded. Could she survive if Cameron left?

Hell, what was wrong with her? She could go with him. Skye could handle the café.

"And you've been stewing about it all this time?"

Kristen ducked her head, nodding. "Yes. I've...I've been waiting for you to tell me. I don't understand. Why would you leave me?"

He tipped her head up, surprising her with the intensity of his gaze. "Do you remember what I said before we walked into that room today?"

Kristen nodded. Since they'd left his parents' place, all she could think about were those three little words. Did he really mean them?

"I. Love. You." He punctuated each word with a kiss. "Never doubt that."

"I love you, too," she whispered.

"About time you admitted it." He cupped her chin and took her lips in a hard kiss.

She opened her mouth to his questing tongue. They tasted, teased and tempted each other. Both were breathing heavily when the kiss ended.

Cameron gazed down at her. "After the scene when Jack had asked me, I wasn't sure what I was going to do. But I knew I was falling for you. What we have goes beyond the kink."

"It does." Her heart swelled with her love for him.

"About a week after our scene, I realized I didn't want to go back to Scotland, at least not without you. But you have a business here."

She opened her mouth to say she'd follow him anywhere.

He placed his fingers against her lips. "A business I would never ask you to give up. My family is here, my teaching is here, and Jack just asked me to become a partner in Decadence."

"What?"

Cameron gave her that devil-may-care smile of his. "The club is growing, and because I enjoy teaching, he offered me a job. I'll still be teaching at the university, but I'll cut back my schedule."

"Are you sure?" For the first time in her life, she found a man willing to put her first. It scared her.

"Yes. Scotland was a good place for me to heal. But I'm home now. With you."

"Oh, Cameron." Tears filled her eyes. She was so happy.

"And this isn't the way I planned it, but, Kristen Caldwell, will you become my wife?"

She laughed. "Yes." She kissed his lips. "Yes, yes, yes." Each word was punctuated by a kiss.

Laughing, he slipped his hand behind her neck on the last kiss.

"Now that that's settled…" He expertly flipped her from leaning on his shoulder to over his knees. "I owe you a punishment for not telling me your fears and concerns."

"Yes, Sir." Kristen grinned. She'd gladly take this punishment, because he was right. She'd never hide anything from him again.

Epilogue

Six months later, Cameron stood at the altar in the small church, waiting. A grin spread over his lips. Kristen was worth waiting for.

After the craziness with her parents, the café hadn't been the same. Busier than ever, Kristen was forced to hire more people. Skye had developed a talent for baking, relieving Kristen from doing it all herself.

"Nervous?" Alec asked.

"No." He was anxious to have Kristen to himself. The double doors opened, and his attention shifted. First came the flower girls, then two of the girls who worked at the café, then his sister.

Skye looked beautiful in her flowing, dark-blue gown as she walked down the aisle. Then there was a pause, and The Wedding March started. Cameron couldn't tear his gaze away when his bride-to-be stepped into the doorway with his father.

Kristen wore a beautiful, white gown with a sash made of McMillan tartan. Pride and love swelled in him as she floated down the aisle toward him.

They stopped next to him, and his father turned to Kristen. "If Cameron doesn't treat you right, he'll answer to me." He lifted Kristen's veil and kissed her cheek, then placed her hand in Cameron's before taking a seat.

"You are so gorgeous you take my breath away,"

Cameron whispered as they turned toward the minister.

"And you, dear Sir, are so sexy in your kilt," Kristen said.

The minister cleared his throat, and the ceremony began.

Minutes felt like hours to Cameron before the minister finally said, "I now pronounce you husband and wife. You may kiss your bride."

Cameron's lips covered Kristen's, keeping the kiss light and playful. When he lifted his head the minister said, "I present Mr. and Mrs. Cameron McMillan."

The crowd cheered.

Kristen turned to him and asked, "So now that we're married, do I get to see what you wear under your kilt?"

"That, my saucy bride, is a Scotsman's secret, only to be revealed after the couple's first is born."

"I can't wait." Kristen laughed as they started down the aisle together.

A year later, sworn to secrecy, Cameron showed her what he wore beneath his kilt, and Kristen could only smile.

Marie Tuhart

About the Author

Multi-published author Marie Tuhart lives in the beautiful Pacific Northwest with her muse, Penny, a four-pound toy poodle. Marie loves to read and write. When she's not writing, she spends time with family, traveling, and enjoying life.

Join Marie's newsletter, where she gives advanced information on her books, runs contests, and does giveaways just for newsletter readers.

Newsletter:
http://eepurl.com/bmWUZH
Website:
www.marietuhart.com
Twitter:
@marietuhart
Pinterest:
http://www.pinterest.com/marietuhart
Facebook:
https://www.facebook.com/MarieTuhartAuthor/
~*~

To chat with Marie Tuhart and other Wild Rose Press authors of erotic romance, join us at
www.groups.yahoo.com/group/thewilderroses.

Adam

Doms of the Silver Screen Book Two

By Marie Tuhart

Director Adam Bainbridge has one job to do—get the film finished. Something that would be much easier if he weren't in love with the leading lady. Taught to always hide his feelings, he denies the passion and love he feels for his ex-wife. Seeing her every day in the arms of another man is too much for his Dom side to bear. He's always wanted her back in his life, in his bed, and under his command. Too bad she has other ideas that don't include him.

Looking to take her acting career to the next level, Nicki Masters accepts the role of a lifetime. She doesn't count on her ex-husband being the film's director. She'd loved him enough to wait for him once despite the pain they experienced together, and he never returned. Now that she's tried to move on, the sexy Dom wants a second chance. Loving him again would be the biggest challenge of her life. She just doesn't believe she can teach an old Dom new tricks.

Also available
from The Wild Rose Press, Inc.
and major retailers.

Kiltless in Carolina
Real Men Wear Kilts
By Ashantay Peters

Unable to say no to family, photographer Isla McAllister agrees to attend the Highland Games under one condition—no roughing it. She wants a comfy hotel room where she can escape her family's matchmaking schemes and avoid her ex-fiancé? Her plans go awry when she discovers her room has been given to a hot highlander with a smile that resurrects forgotten fantasies. Unfortunately, he's a kilt-wearing piper, just like her ex.

After a bad breakup, Graeme MacKay plans on getting laid during the Games. He's gone too long with his bagpipes as the only instrument getting any play. His number one criteria for the woman who'll share his bed—she has to be a non-Scot. But when he clashes with a feisty MacAllister who claims he stole her room, he throws caution to the wind and offers to share his room…and his bed.

Thank you for purchasing this
publication of The Wild Rose Press, Inc.
If you enjoyed the story, we would appreciate
your letting others know by leaving a review.

For questions or more
information contact us at
info@thewildrosepress.com.

Stay current with The Wild Rose Press, Inc.
Like us on Facebook
https://www.facebook.com/TheWildRosePress
And Follow us on Twitter
https://twitter.com/WildRosePress